Callie's Rules

Callie's Rules

NAOMI ZUCKER

EGMONT
USA

NEW YORK

EGMONT

We bring stories to life

First published by Egmont USA, 2009
443 Park Avenue South, Suite 806
New York, NY 10016

1 3 5 7 9 8 6 4 2

www.egmontusa.com
www.naomizucker.net

Library of Congress Cataloging-in-Publication Data

Zucker, Naomi Flink.
Callie's rules / by Naomi Zucker.
p. cm.
Summary: Eleven-year-old Callie Jones tries to keep track of all the rules for fitting in that other middle schoolers seems to know, but when the town decides to replace Halloween with an Autumn Festival, Callie leads her large family in an unusual protest.
ISBN 978-1-60684-027-6 (hardcover) — ISBN 978-1-60684-052-8 (lib. bdg. ed.)
[1. Rules (Philosophy)—Fiction. 2. Individuality—Fiction. 3. Middle schools—Fiction.
4. Schools—Fiction. 5. Family life—New Jersey—Fiction. 6. Halloween—Fiction.
7. New Jersey—Fiction.] I. Title.
PZ7.Z7795Cal 2009
[Fic]—dc22
2009015419

Interior text design by Joann Hill

Printed in the United States of America

For Raphaella

And for Isaac and Zalman

●　●　●　●　●

Callie's Rules

1 Wardrobes and Weirdos

"Calliope Jones?"

There it is—my name, my very own name, a name that only a mother like mine would bestow on an innocent baby. I can't even blame my fate on a wicked fairy godmother. It was all my mother's doing. My father wanted to call me Jane. But no, it had to be Calliope. I was doomed at birth.

I shoot my hand up, knocking my *Jane Eyre* to the floor. When I reach down to grab it, I smash my elbow against the corner of my desk. And here it comes, right on cue, Shane Belcher's falsetto: "Cuh-lie-oh-pee, can I go pee?"

I would turn and give Shane a death stare, but my eyes are teared up from the elbow smack.

Of course, all the boys have to repeat what Shane said. They whisper so the teacher won't hear, but then they all start laughing. Mrs. Thigpen looks toward the back of the room, where all the boys are, narrows her eyes, and, one by one, freezes them with icicle eyes. They stop laughing.

"Please call me Callie, Mrs. Thigpen." Why did my voice come out sounding so puny?

"Oh, do you pronounce it *Caa*-lee-ope? I thought you'd been named for the Greek muse of poetry."

Oh, good grief! This is turning into the Salem witch trials. Death by drowning would be less painful.

"You said it right."

"Correctly. I did not say it right. I said it correctly. You do pronounce your name Calliope."

Like a chorus, a whining Greek chorus, all the boys chant, "Can I go pee?" But softly so the teacher won't hear.

Mrs. Thigpen has a bulging forehead and a disappearing chin; when she turns to the side, she looks as if she should have been attached to the prow of a sailing ship. Now she announces, in a voice like a foghorn, "Calliope, class, was the eldest Muse, and was also called the 'Fair Voiced.' When she is depicted, she holds in her hand a writing tablet and she is crowned in gold."

I never thought I'd be grateful to Valeri Van Dine for anything at all, but when she just then appears in the doorway, beaming her thank-you-all-for-coming-today smile, Mrs. Thigpen forgets about me and watches Valeri sashay slowly to an empty seat.

Doesn't she look perfect? Alyce writes on a slip of paper and passes it to me. (Alyce Kane is my best friend. She used to be Alice until the summer, when she decided that for middle school Alice was too babyish and she started spelling her name Alyce.)

Who? I write back. As if I don't know.

Valeri, of course.

I don't know. She looks the same as always to me.

I mean the scarf she's wearing. It's so cool.

Is that what it is? A scarf? It looks like a boa constrictor wound itself around her neck. And how can you say it's cool? It must be over eighty degrees today!

Oh, Callie, don't you know anything? All the celebrities are wearing them. I think we should get some scarves and wear them just like that.

I will, Alyce. In December.

Alyce shoots me a you-don't-know-anything look. I think maybe she's right.

While Mrs. Thigpen finishes calling the roll, I write *Valeri Van Dine* at the top of the last page of my notebook. Then underneath it I write:

EVIL
VAIN
VILE
DEVIL
DEVIL IN A RAVEN

That last one uses every letter in her name. It doesn't make much sense, but I like it anyway.

Mrs. Thigpen has finished calling the roll. She's handing out the books. One of the books is a novel—*Lorna Doone.* We've never read a grown-up novel in school before; maybe middle school will turn out all right. I skip the preface—I don't read prefaces until sometime after I've read the book, and only if I really liked it—and start with chapter one.

If anybody cares to read a simple tale told simply, I, John Ridd, of the parish of Oare, in the county of Somerset, yeoman and

*churchwarden, have seen and had a share
in some doings of this neighborhood, which
I will try to set down in order, God sparing
my life and memory. And they who light
upon this book should bear in mind not
only that I write for the clearing of our parish from ill fame and calumny . . .*

That's it. I'm done. Anybody else might care to read this "simple tale," but not me. I'll read *Jane Eyre* instead; now there's a book that pulls you right in.

Mrs. T is asking us to put away our books and pay attention. I guess I'd better. Now she's telling us that she wants us to write down in our notebooks what we're learning each day. Okay, I can do that.

Tuesday, September 8

What I Learned Today:

1. If all the celebrities decide to look like they're being strangled by boa constrictors, then I should, too.
2. Fashion that's "cool" can be very hot to wear.

That's it. That's all I've learned today. No, now that I think about it, I learned one other thing.

3. Don't ride your bike to middle school.

I didn't want to be late for school today, on the first day of middle school, so I rode my bike. First day, first mistake. Everyone was standing around, waiting for the doors to open. I didn't see a bike rack anywhere, so I asked an older girl. She gave me a funny look and told me to go around to the back. When I found the rack and locked up my bike, I saw why she'd given me that look—my bike was the only one there.

I guess riding a bike to school is like spelling your name with an *i*—too babyish for middle school. I wonder if it would help if I started to spell my name Callye. No, that's just too weird, even for me. It looks like a word that belongs in *Lorna Doone*.

I'm pretty sure this is not what Mrs. T meant when she asked us to write down what we're learning, but they haven't started teaching us anything yet, so those three things are all I've learned. Well, those things and that I won't be reading *Lorna Doone.*

It turns out that Alyce and I have the same lunch period—second lunch—and by now I'm starving. I've gulped down half my sandwich before I even look around. All the other girls have taken their phones out of their purses and they're passing them around to show their pictures.

"Oh, look, that's us at the beach."

"Who's that cute boy?"

"I remember when we took this one."

I'm the only one eating. I take out my notebook and add two more things to my list:

4. Have lots of pictures in your phone to show at lunch.
5. Don't eat lunch.

Looking at my list, it seems that all the things I've learned are rules. Stupid rules. Well, rules are rules. They're not supposed to make sense. They're supposed to make the people who know the rules feel good and the people who don't know the rules feel stupid. The rules may be stupid, but the list idea isn't bad. I start another one.

Callie's Rules. Things to Do:

- Get lots of pictures in your phone.
- Get a phone.
- Get a purse.

And then I think of one more list.

Callie's Rules. Why It's Better to Be a Boy:

- Boys don't have to worry about what they wear.
- Boys get to eat lunch.

That was my last list. I promise. Maybe.

After school, I walk Alyce home. When we get into town, we stop in front of Cubby's. Over the summer, when most people were away, Alyce and I went to Cubby's nearly every day. Alyce likes her Coke with a squirt of cherry; I prefer lemon and lime. Today, it looks like the entire school is jammed in there, drinking Cokes and eating fries.

Valeri is perched at the edge of a front booth, seven or eight girls squeezed in with her. Alyce and I keep on walking, out of town.

People in Hillcrest call the four or five blocks where the stores are "town." They say, "We're going into town," as though they're going to hitch the horse to the buckboard and ride for eight or ten miles. When you get past the movie theater, you're "out of town."

Alyce's house is at the end of Hillcrest Avenue. All the time we're walking there, Alyce is going on about school, the clothes everyone was wearing, and a cute boy who has all the same classes she has, and where do I think we can get really cool scarves like the one Valeri was wearing. When we get to Alyce's house, she says, "Callie, there's so much to talk about. Why don't I walk you back to your house? We can go to your room and talk there."

"We can't. You know I don't have my own room. I have to share with my sister and we can't really talk or anything when she's in there. Mel's a blabbermouth. She'll ask you a hundred questions and she'll have told the whole town what you said before you even get home. I'll see you in school tomorrow."

That's a lie—not the room part, but the part about Mel—and not even a good lie, but right now, I don't really want to be talking to Alyce. She's different than she used to be. Maybe it started when she changed the way she spelled her name. She used to hate Valeri as much as I did. Now she thinks Valeri is cool. She even wants to dress like her. For Pete's sake, Alyce even knows what the celebrities are wearing! How does she know these things? I sure don't.

I take off before Alyce can say anything. But I know what she's thinking. She's thinking I'm weird. Maybe I am, but I'm not half as weird as my parents. Or my house.

No one is in the house when I get home, so I walk out the kitchen door to the backyard. The double doors to the shed are open. It's dark inside the shed except for flashes of blue light, flickering off eyeless faces—grinning, scowling, leering, metal faces.

When my eyes adjust to the dark, I pick my way across the bits of scrap metal and wire that litter the shed floor.

"Callie! You came home."

That's my baby sister Polly. Everyone calls her Polly—everyone, that is, except my mother, who insists on calling her Polyhymnia. I lean over the top of Polly's wooden cage and kiss her cloud of light brown hair.

"Hi, Polly. What are you making?"

"A castle. For the weirdo to live in."

"She means the one I've started." The voice echoes, as if it's coming from inside a cave. "Come and see." That's my mother speaking from behind a welder's mask. With the visor pulled down over her face, and wearing a thick gray vest and heavy gauntlets, she looks like a medieval knight. She's holding a welder's torch that's shooting a blue flame, like a fire-breathing dragon.

I can just imagine what Alyce thinks of my mother. Alyce's mother is normal. She wears aprons with sayings on them, like QUEEN OF THE KITCHEN. For Valentine's Day, she has an apron with pink hearts on it and she has about a dozen different aprons for Christmas. The only flames she even comes close to are the ones on her kitchen stove. In summer, when they barbecue, Alyce's father is the one who starts the fire. He says men have been making fires ever since caveman days.

Mr. Kane has a sort of a cave of his own. Well, it's really a survival shelter, but it looked to me like a cave. Most of the basements I've seen have rec rooms in them, with Foosball tables. But the Kanes have a survival shelter.

Last summer, Alyce took me down to their basement to show me the shelter. Mr. Kane built it himself. Alyce explained about the air blower and the filter (to protect against radiation). There were even packaged meals and water, enough to last two weeks. Alyce said Mr. Kane is going to get survival suits for the three of them. Then she said, "Callie, you mustn't tell anyone about this shelter. If people find out about this, when the terrorists strike, other people will want us to take them in. We can't. There won't be room or enough food. But Callie, if there's an attack, I want you to come. Just don't tell anyone else. Okay?"

Alyce was quiet for a while. Then she said, "And Callie, when you come, maybe you could bring some food for yourself. Freeze-dried, of course."

I said okay, and I meant it—at least the part

about not telling anyone else. But I didn't mean it about me going in to the shelter with Alyce. I just didn't think I'd want to live in a world where my family, all the animals, the trees, and the plants were dead. The Kanes might be safe, but everything I care about will be barbecued.

My father would never barbecue because he won't eat meat. I'll spare you his lectures on cruelty to animals. It really almost puts you off ever eating meat again. Almost.

"Calliope?" My mother turns off her torch and raises her visor. "Calliope, I asked you a question. How was your first day of middle school?"

"All right, I guess."

"Just all right? Who are your teachers? How do they seem?"

"They're fine. My teachers are fine. Everything was just fine."

My mother doesn't say anything, just looks at me, trying to see inside my head.

"So, what's this weirdo going to be?"

My mother twists her mouth a little. "Calliope, you're not answering my question. How was school?"

"I did answer, Mom. It was fine. But you're not answering mine—what's this weirdo going to be?"

My mother lowers her visor. One good thing about my mother, she knows when to give up.

"I'm not sure. I just started cutting and soldering. This weirdo will tell me what it wants to be. I only know that this one is going to be very tall. For now, I'm calling it Number Eighteen."

Numbers One through Seventeen are standing like sentries along the back wall. They're all sizes—fat, thin, tall, short. They snarl or smile. Some of them have lights inside, and they glow yellow from their eyes and noses and mouths. One of them blows blue smoke from its ears. And another rattles its teeth when the wind blows.

I love those weirdos. We all do. They're for Halloween. The weekend before, the whole family, even little Polly, helps haul the weirdos out of the shed. There are seven of us kids. Jack's the oldest, then my sister Andy (Andromeda to my mother), then me and my sister Mel (Melpomene), the twins, Ted and Fred, and, of course, Polly (Polyhymnia to my mother). You must have noticed that the three boys have normal names. It was my father who got to name all the boys. My parents still argue about it. My mother insists that Jack, Ted, and Fred aren't names at all; they're nicknames. To which my father always says that nicknames are what people will call the boys for the rest of their lives, so why bother giving them names they'll never use. My father also says that the boys will save a lot of ink over their lifetimes. With seven kids, my father worries a lot about saving money.

The nine of us stagger across the front yard— some of those weirdos are pretty heavy—crunching the dry leaves under our feet, stomping on the brittle branches of the wildflowers that we have in our yard instead of grass. My father marks out a snaking path from the sidewalk to our front door and we set up the weirdos alongside.

It takes hours. When we're done, we're all pretty tired. And also pretty nuts. Last year, when all the weirdos were set up, my brother Jack decided we should do the bunny hop in and out of the line of weirdos. We were having a great time, hopping, laughing, and then I saw Mrs. Farkas, our neighbor, who'd come out on her front porch, I guess to see what all the noise was about. There was a look on her face—disbelief, disgust, disapproval, maybe all of those things at the same time. I felt like a last-summer's beach ball, with all the air squished out of me. I ran up to my room.

2 Pumpkins and Paintings and Dragons

The thing is, I really love those weirdos. And I love that my mother can dream them up, and I'm proud that she can cut the metal and weld it—she taught herself all of that. It's just that our way of doing Halloween is so different from everybody else's. Nobody in town has anything the least bit like a weirdo. They buy all their Halloween decorations.

And everyone else buys a pumpkin, maybe with a face painted on it, or they carve a smiley face and put the pumpkin out on the front porch. But not us. Oh no. We can't even do jack-o'-lanterns like other people's. My father grows his own pumpkins. All summer, he's growing his pumpkins. And he sings to them. He does. He sings, "Grow little pumpkin, bigger, bigger. Grow little pumpkin, plump your figure. When you gotta grow, you gotta grow. Grow little pumpkin, grow." It's to the tune of "Glow Little Glow Worm." He makes us kids water the pumpkins with him and, even worse, he always makes us sing to them. I'm glad he grows his pumpkins in the *back*yard.

A couple of days before Halloween, he picks out the biggest pumpkin, hollows it out, and carves a face in it. Okay, that's sort of like everyone else, except that he doesn't just put a flashlight in his pumpkin, he lights a regular fire in it and calls it a cauldron. The other fathers stay inside and when you ring their doorbells, they open the front door and make little cooing noises about how cute the kids look and hand out little wrapped candies. Some people give out apples. (No kid ever wants the apples. The next day the whole town smells like applesauce.)

But that's not how my father does it. No, he stands right outside the house, wearing a ghoul costume, next to his "cauldron," and when the trick-or-treaters come to the end of the trail of weirdos, Father calls out, "Come and get your Toasty Ghosties. No charge. Free for this one night. Nothing better on Halloween than a mass of ectoplasm, on top of a flattened bat, between two coffin lids." The ectoplasm is melted marshmallows, the flattened bat a square of chocolate, and the coffin lids two graham crackers. The Toasty Ghosties are really just s'mores. But I love them.

I love the Toasty Ghosties. And I love my mother's weirdos. And I hate that I wish that my mother, my father, our Halloween were like everyone else's. It's like I'm two different people. Behold! The Dread Calliope Schizoid! By day, she's an eleven-year-old girl who follows the rules—once she catches on to them. But by night—aha, by night!—she turns as weird as her parents.

And while we're on the subject of weird—what is this thing that my mother has prepared for dinner? It's something brown wrapped in green leaves. I won't eat anything I can't put a name to, but everyone's talking at once and no one answers me when I ask what it's called. So I grab an ear of corn as the bowl whizzes past me and with my other hand snatch a roll from across the table. The butter's at the other end and I have to get up and walk around the table to get it.

Our table—that's another weird thing. It came

from a monastery. My mother says the table has a history and that gives it character. I wonder if the monks were the kind who take a vow of silence. If they were, what would they think if they came into the room right now? I imagine a line of them in their brown robes, their sandals shuffling across the floor. When they hear all of us talking, they wince and put their fingers to their lips. Then, without a word, they pile our glasses, forks, and knives onto our plates, hand them to us, pick up the table, and carry it away. Leaving all of us sitting in our chairs, speechless, tableless, holding our plates in the air.

Suddenly, Polly's piping voice breaks through. It's amazing how she can make herself heard when she wants to. It must be because her voice is so high.

"Be quiet! I want to say something."

Everyone stops talking.

"I want to tell you that Mommy started a weirdo today. It's for Halloween."

"Do you even know what Halloween is?" That's Jack, teasing her. I wish he wouldn't do that.

"Yes, I do." Polly doesn't let anyone put her down. "I remember from last year. I remember everything. Mommy says she'll make me a lion suit to go with my furry lion slippers. I'm going to growl."

"Lions don't growl, they roar." Jack again. I wish he'd stop.

"You don't know." Polly climbs up on her chair, still holding her fork. "I saw a lion once in the backyard and he was growling."

"There are no lions in New Jersey. Except in zoos."

"That's enough, Jack," my mother says. Polly looks as if she's going to cry. "If Polyhymnia's lion wants to growl, she can."

"My lion is a boy lion."

"Oh, I didn't know. Well then, *he* can growl if he wants to."

Mel is sitting across from me, and I know the look on her face, that looking-right-at-you-but-not-seeing-you look. Mel's an artist, and I can tell she's started planning her window painting. The window painting is one of the best things about living in this town. Each school runs a contest for the best Halloween pictures. The art teachers pick the winners, and on the day before Halloween, all the elementary-school kids get the afternoon off and the winning artists draw their pictures on the store windows. The rest of us kids paint them in. I hope Mel's picture gets chosen. And I hope it doesn't rain afterward. When it rains, all the paint dribbles off the glass onto the sidewalk.

The window painting isn't the only good thing about Halloween in Hillcrest. There's a parade, too. All of us kids march through town, in our costumes, between the painted windows, through the park, and into the high school, where we walk across the stage. Afterward, the mothers of the Parents' Association ladle out paper cups of cider and hand us doughnuts tucked into paper napkins. The little kids get powdered sugar all over their painted faces.

I love that costume parade. Though I have to say that we don't even do costumes like everybody else. Everybody else buys theirs. We make our own. But I don't care. For one night, inside my costume, even if it's the only one that's homemade, I'm just like everyone else. It doesn't matter if my costume is different; it's supposed to be. For that one night, I'm not Calliope Jones, I'm just a kid in a costume.

Ted suddenly yells out, "Waca," and Fred starts

grinning and nodding, and he says, "Ey." I should explain about the twins—they have their own language. They started when they were babies. My mother said it was baby talk and they'd outgrow it. But they didn't. I said it was because the rest of us were talking all the time and didn't let them get a word in. So for a week, we all kept absolutely quiet when we were with the twins, didn't say a single word. That was creepy. But it didn't work. Even when the rest of us weren't saying a word, the twins would just keep on talking to each other in their twin talk. It took a while, but my father figured out that they understood English perfectly well, they just liked to pretend they didn't. And even better, they could understand what we were saying, but we couldn't understand them. Pretty smart!

"Boys"—that's my father—"please use your proper words."

"A cow," Ted explains. "We're going to be a cow."

"In a sheet," Fred adds. "With black spots."

"I'll be the head," Ted says, "because I'm taller, and Fred will be the back end."

Suddenly, I have an idea—a beautiful, glorious,

Fourth-of-July-fireworks of an idea, an idea so big it bursts right out of me.

"A dragon! A Chinese dragon! For our costume. All of us. One long Chinese dragon, with all seven of us inside. Well, six anyway. Polly's too young. We can make a papier-mâché head and a frame for the body. We can paint the body with neon colors. Flashing eyes. A swishing tail."

"Callie, we can't all be a dragon." That's my sister Andy.

"Why not, Andy? It'll work, I know it'll work. I can see the whole thing."

"It's a good idea, Callie, but we can't do it. There won't be enough kids."

"Why not?"

"Because"—and now Andy sounds like she's talking to Polly—"because high-school kids don't wear costumes in the parade. Jack and I are in high school."

Well, la-dee-dah. The great ones are too important to wear a costume with us little kids. That's it, I'm leaving.

"Calliope, where are you going? Sit down and finish your dinner."

"I *am* finished. And so is my idea. I'm going to my room."

I don't even have a "my room." I have half a room. I flop down on my bed and start to read *Jane Eyre*. Right now, I want to forget me. I want to be Jane. Bad things happen to her, really bad things, but it all comes out right at the end. It always does in books. I haven't read more than a page when Polly slips in the door and climbs up next to me. I can't be alone anywhere in this house.

"Read to me, Callie."

"You wouldn't like this book. It's got big words and no pictures."

"I don't care. I want you to read me your book."

Polly will just keep pestering me until I read to her. She never gives up. "Okay. I'll read you my book: 'We must decontaminate the deckle,' said the Doberman pinscher. 'The judgment of the judiciary is upon us. But first, let me compose a roulade upon my piccolo.'"

"That's not what it says, Callie. Read me the real book."

"You don't believe me? Here, read it for yourself."

"You know I can't read."

"Well, then, you'll just have to take my word for it. Do you want me to read more?"

"No. That's a stupid book."

Polly skips out, but then Andy strolls in and plops down on my bed.

"What do *you* want?"

"Don't be mad, Callie. After you left, we thought about your suggestion, about us all being a Chinese dragon."

"Okay, so it was a stupid idea. Can I please read my book now?"

"Wait, Callie. Let me finish. We started talking and I said how this was going to be the last year we're all together for Halloween. Jack will be in college next year. And a couple of years later, I'll be gone. And so we said, why not? Let's have one last Halloween together, the best one we've ever had. We want to make that Chinese dragon. Just the way you described it, with the flashing eyes, the tail. It'll be great, Callie."

People can surprise you. They're not always what you think. Like Andy. She's really pretty, with shiny black hair and green eyes. Of course she's popular. And she knows all the rules. She always knows what she's supposed to wear. You wouldn't expect that she's a really nice person. But she is. People aren't always what you expect them to be.

3 Futile Fridays

"Settle down, class. I don't want to have to ask twice."

Mrs. Thigpen has the kind of voice that doesn't need to ask twice. If she were a gym teacher, she wouldn't need a whistle.

"In a few minutes, class, Principal Nolan will be coming in to speak to us. What he has to say is quite important, and I expect you to give him your full attention."

Great. We're going to get the pep talk about how everyone at the school is here to help us and his door is always open. And there he is, opening the door. Mr. Nolan—I guess that's who this must be—is astoundingly tall and lanky. He doesn't so much walk into the room as stretch himself into it. If he were in the circus, they'd call him the Human

Rubber Band. He coils himself onto the edge of Mrs. Thigpen's desk.

"Good morning, class. I'm Principal Nolan. My job is to help the teachers and to help you make the most of your years at Hillcrest Middle School. Remember that my door is always open to you."

I slide *Jane Eyre* onto my lap and start reading. But then I hear the word *test* and I put the book away.

". . . system-wide tests will be administered this spring."

This is everyone's cue to groan, and I groan right along with them. It's not that I hate tests. I don't. I actually like them. For me, they're sort of a contest, like some kids want to get chosen first for a team, or be the most popular. Neither of those things is ever going to happen to me. I just know I can do really well on tests. Some distinction, huh! Anyway, I groan with everybody else and try to look really unhappy.

"I see that some of you have already heard about the tests, and you probably have some questions about what they will mean for you. I can tell you that these examinations will mean a great deal—

not only for you students but for the school system as a whole. Our reputation, the reputation of our town, rests on your performance. Next May, every student in every grade will be tested in the basic subjects. Any student who does not receive a score of seventy or better in a subject will have to repeat the course in a summer program. But we don't want that, and I'm sure you don't. I want every student in this school to perform well."

Hands are shooting up all over the room.

"One moment, please. Let me finish, and then I'll answer your questions. As I was saying, these tests mean a great deal for the school. We want to be known as a school that succeeds. We all do want to succeed, don't we?"

Everyone is looking blank.

"I can see that you do. And we must all work very hard to make that happen. Now your teacher, Mrs. Thigpen, and all the other teachers over the summer have been developing a program that will prepare you for the tests in May. We will be devoting every Friday to test preparation."

Well, I won't be calling them Fun-Filled Fridays.

"You will work through a series of specific units;

in the fall, those units will be . . ." Mr. Nolan pulls some index cards out of his pocket and shuffles through them until he finds the one he's looking for. "In the fall, those units will be grammar, sentence structure, punctuation, and spelling."

More specifically, they'll be Fundamentals Fridays. The kids are squirming, still shooting up their hands. Mr. Nolan doesn't seem to notice.

"You must pass one unit before you can proceed to the next. If you successfully pass every unit this fall, then in the spring you will move on to more advanced areas, such as finding the main idea in a paragraph, arranging ideas in order, and drawing conclusions."

All around me more hands are springing up like mushrooms.

"I can see that you have a lot of questions, but I have to speak to the other classes, so I'll let Mrs. Thigpen answer them. Thank you." Mr. Nolan unrolls himself and slides out the door.

Wetherly, who is sitting in the front row and waving her hand wildly, doesn't even wait to be called on.

"Mrs. Thigpen, Mrs. Thigpen."

"Yes, Wetherly, do you have a question or are you merely trying to circulate the air in this room?"

"No—I mean, yes. I mean, I do have a question. How are we supposed to pass this test? I mean, it doesn't seem fair. We've never taken these tests before. How are we supposed to know what questions will be on them?"

Maybe, in Wetherly's honor, I'll name today Thick-Headed Thursday.

"I believe, Wetherly," Mrs. Thigpen says, "that that is the purpose of a test. If we tell you the questions in advance, it will hardly be a test at all, will it? If you will just allow your hand a bit of a rest, Wetherly, I'll explain further.

"As Mr. Nolan told you, every Friday will be devoted to preparation for a single unit on the tests. Before you begin working on a unit, you will be given a pretest. No, Wetherly, the grade on this pretest won't 'count.' That is what you were about to ask, wasn't it? When you've taken the pretest, I will correct it and then you will have a clear idea of which areas you need to work on. I'll then give you a series of worksheets for that area. When you feel ready, you can take another pretest, and if you pass it, you can move on to the next unit. Is that clear?"

Wetherly looks more confused than usual. "What if we take the pretest a second time and we still don't pass?"

Mrs. Thigpen sighs. "Then you will keep on working until you do pass. Or, in May, fail."

Right. Wetherly might as well resign herself to Futile Fridays.

The next morning, all anyone can talk about are the tests. Valeri is chirping, "What if I fail? I couldn't sleep at all last night, just worrying about it." Valeri knows she won't fail. She may be evil, but she's not stupid. She just likes the attention. And she gets lots of it.

Alyce is dumping the entire contents of her purse onto her desk—wallet, comb, Lifesavers, wadded-up tissues, bus pass. "Oh, no. I haven't got a pencil. How am I going to take the pretest without a pencil?" Her hands are shaking.

"Here, Alyce. I have extras."

Mrs. T takes a stack of booklets from her desk. "No talking, class. Now, please remove all books and papers from your desks. You should have only a pencil."

Alyce gives me a weak smile of thanks.

I glance through my booklet; it's only three pages long and it's all multiple choice. You have to look at each sentence and find the mistake in grammar. Everyone around me is hunched over their desks, clenching their pencils. I barely have to read the sentences. I just flick my eyes over them, and right away I spot the errors. I'm finished in only a few minutes.

I'm finished all right. What am I supposed to do now? Most of the period is still left. I can't take out my book and read; Mrs. T asked us to clear our desks. I can't even write. I've messed up. Again.

"Calliope, would you step up to my desk, please?"

Oh great, now everybody's looking at me. I can still feel their eyes on my back when I'm standing at the teacher's desk.

"Calliope." Mrs. T is talking softly. The other kids might be looking at us, but at least they won't hear. "Calliope, you seem to be having some difficulty with the pretest. What is the problem?"

"No problem, Mrs. Thigpen. I finished and I wasn't sure what to do next."

"You finished." She sounds as if she doesn't believe me.

"Yes. And there's still a lot of time left and—"

"I see. Well, bring me your pretest and let me look it over. While I'm doing that, why don't you try the next test, sentence structure."

Walking back, I don't have to imagine everyone staring at me—I can *see* them staring at me. Well, what was I supposed to do? Mrs. T called me to her desk, it wasn't my idea.

I finish the sentence-structure test pretty quickly, too, and then the one for punctuation. By the time I bring Mrs. T the last pretest, the one for spelling, I'm hot and sweating. This is beginning to feel like the walk to the electric chair. Except I could really use someone walking alongside praying for me.

Before I sit down, I glance around the room. No one's looking at me. They're all staring at their tests. Everyone except Shane Belcher. He's lolling back in his seat, his long finger rubbing back and forth on his lower lip, gazing up at the ceiling. He looks as though he's mulling over a question, but he's not. He's stalling! That's what Shane is doing, stalling! He's taking his time so he won't be finished ahead of everyone else.

The way I was. The way I was four times. I didn't just finish one test ahead of everybody else, I finished all four of them. I must be the biggest drip that ever slid down the drain.

"Time is up, class." Mrs. T moves down the aisles, collecting the tests. Her thick square heels ring as they strike the wooden floor. The chimes of doom. When she gets to my desk, she stops. "Please stay a moment, Calliope. I'd like to speak with you."

It's not over yet. Before they scramble out of the room, every kid stops and stares at me. Every kid except Shane Belcher. He's probably congratulating himself on being a lot smarter than me. Well, I've got news for him—that isn't hard.

"Calliope, I haven't graded your spelling test yet, but you've passed all the others. More than passed. You made only two errors—both on the punctuation test. I don't quite know what to do about this. It would be a waste of your time for you to go on with these units. You should pass the final test quite easily. So for now, I'll excuse you from test preparation on Fridays. You can use the time to work on your other class assignments."

I try to keep my face serious when I thank Mrs. T, but inside me a voice is shouting, *Free Fridays! Free Fridays!*

Callie's Rules for Tests:

- When you take a test, take your time. The worst thing in the world is to be finished ahead of everybody else.
- The first rule doesn't really matter because from now on I'll have Fridays free.
- The first rule does matter. I only want to believe that it doesn't.

4 The American Way

After school, I tell Alyce that I can't walk her home today, my mother needs me for something. I want some time alone, and time alone isn't something I get a lot of. Not with school all day and seven kids at home and me sharing a bedroom. If I go straight home, I'll have an hour. My mother will be back in the shed, working on her weirdo; Polly will be in her cage; Jack will be at his job at the market; Andy helps out at the animal shelter on Fridays; and all the younger kids get out of school an hour later.

I'm planning to load up a plate with food, flop on my bed, and stare at the ceiling. I don't even want to read, just eat and stare at the ceiling.

I've just opened the refrigerator when the front doorbell rings. Great, just great! Probably someone selling tickets to a ham-and-bean supper. Except the woman standing on the other side of the door doesn't look like she's ever even been to a ham-and-bean supper. She's perfect. Her light brown hair gleams like a scoop of chocolate ice cream. She's wearing a silky coral blouse with matching lipstick. The only way this woman would be selling anything would be on the pages of a magazine.

"Hi," the perfect woman purrs. "Is your mother at home? I'm Sandy Van Dine."

"Um, yeah, I think so. I have to go check."

Um, yeah, I think so? Did I really say that? Hello, perfect person, meet the town doofus. I'm slinking to the back door when it hits me. Van Dine! The woman said her name is Van Dine. She must be Valeri's mother. If she sees my mother, if she sees our house . . . By tonight, she'll have told Valeri all about us, and by tomorrow, Valeri will have blabbed to everyone in school. Valeri spreads bad things around like a cold in kindergarten.

Why did I say I'd get my mother? I could have said that my mother wasn't home, that she was at the dentist, or away at a family reunion or something. But no, I not only had to sound like a hick, I had to say I'd go check. I can go back and say I checked and my mother's not home. But then that Van Dine person will only come back another time. I might as well go outside and get my mother.

Outside! I've left the woman standing on the front step. I race back to the front door. "Mrs. Van Dine, I'm so sorry. Where are my manners? Won't you come in?"

Where are my manners? Now I'm talking like Scarlet O'Hara! I leave Mrs. Van Dine standing inside the front door and rush to the back door and jerk the cowbell. That's the signal for all the kids to come home from wherever they are. Right now, it's the signal for my mother to come in from the shed. With the cowbell echoing in my ears, I race back to Mrs. Van Dine.

And then I stand there, not having the slightest idea what to say. I've already probably convinced her that I'm some sort of mental case. The best thing I can do now is just shut up. We're standing there, the two of us, me not saying anything and Mrs. Van Dine with a little set smile, trying very hard to look as though everything around her is as perfect as she is.

It seems like an hour before my mother makes an appearance. And she does make an appearance. Her gray-streaked hair is tied back with a piece of string, and longish strands are clinging to her sweat-shiny face. She's wearing an old shirt of my father's, overalls specked with bits of solder, and work boots. Polly trails behind her, holding my mother's leg with one hand and sucking the thumb of the other.

Mrs. Van Dine is still smiling that set smile. "Hello," she coos, and holds out her hand. Her nail polish is the same color as her lipstick. "I'm Sandy Van Dine."

"Hello. What a lovely name you have. I'm Mary Jones. I'm afraid my name sounds like something in a police file."

Mrs. Van Dine jerks her hand away. "You've been arrested?"

"Of course not." My mother is frowning a little. "I only meant— Oh, never mind. Why don't you come in and sit down. Then we can talk more comfortably."

Well, sure, why not go all the way and give the lady a tour of our house. Then she—and Valeri—

will know it all. But she doesn't need the full tour, the living room's bad enough. Maybe Mrs. Van Dine would like to sit in the barber's chair. My mother found that one day in the parking lot behind a barbershop. My father always says that there's nothing like lying back in a barber's chair, with his feet up, having a scalp massage. So when my mother saw that chair, she had to have it brought home.

And if the barber's chair doesn't suit Mrs. Van Dine (somehow I can't see her lying back and putting her feet up—not in our living room, not anywhere), there's a room full of rocking chairs for her to choose from. Rocking chairs in every size, just like in the three bears' house. Except that they had only three chairs. We probably have a dozen.

Mrs. Van Dine looks over the room as though she's turned up at that ham-and-bean supper and she's looking for something she could possibly eat. Finally, she fixes on a middle-size rocking chair. She perches on the edge of the seat, crosses her ankles, and places her purse on the table next to her. Maybe she won't notice that the bottom of the table used to be a birdbath and the top of the table was an instrument tray from a dentist's office. You'd never guess, unless you looked at it closely and saw that the rim of the tray looks like a ring of tiny teeth.

My mother sits down opposite the woman, and Polly crawls into her lap.

"I believe you've met my daughter Calliope. And this is my daughter Polyhymnia."

"What interesting names." *Interesting*—a polite word for strange. "And how lovely that you have two daughters."

"Actually, I have four. And three sons."

Mrs. Van Dyne's eyes widen just a bit. "How perfectly . . . original."

Original. That's another polite word. I'll have to remember that one. I'm Callie, I'm original.

"I do try to be original. I work as an artist."

"You work. As an artist. I must say, I admire you. I'm afraid I've never had a career. Whatever free time I've had, I've devoted to community and volunteer work. And then every Wednesday afternoon, I help out at the thrift shop. I do feel that those of us who are more fortunate should help those who have less."

I know that look on my mother's face. It's the look she gets when she and my father are paying the bills.

"How can I help you, Sandy?"

My mother's being super polite.

"I really hope you can, Mary. I've been giving a lot of thought lately to Halloween."

"Really? So have we. Just last night the children were planning their costumes."

"Were they? Well, you know, it's precisely the children's costumes that I'm concerned about."

"Concerned? Is it their safety that worries you? You needn't worry about my brood. We've told them only to go to the houses of people they know. And they won't wear masks that cover their eyes, and they'll carry flashlights. I'm sure they'll be safe."

"It's not their physical safety I'm worried about—although, of course, that's important. I'm worried about the safety of their minds."

The safety of our minds? Does she think that Halloween is going to drive us crazy? That we'll be howling like werewolves? Or trying to fly out of our bedroom windows on our broomsticks? What's she talking about?

"I'm afraid I don't understand," my mother says. So I'm not the only one confused.

"Let me explain, Mary. As you know, Halloween has its origins in pagan beliefs. It has to do with the spirits of the dead, witches, goblins; you know the sort of thing. That all originated, of course, in more primitive times, in Europe. But we're living in America, and this is not the Dark Ages. Those pagan superstitions don't belong here. You must agree that they're, well, they're rather un-American."

"Un-American?" My mother leans forward, pursing her lips and frowning slightly, as though she's trying hard to understand something very serious.

"Yes, un-American. This country was founded under God. Not under gods and demons and devils and who knows what else."

"Witches and goblins. I believe you mentioned those before."

"Yes, I did. I knew you'd understand, Mary."

It's Mrs. Van Dine who doesn't understand. My mother was being ironic.

"If we let our children start down that path, we both know very well where it will lead."

"No, I'm afraid I don't. Where will it lead?'

"Why, to paganism, even satanism."

Mrs. Van Dyne seems to feel that she's said something very important because she nods her head briskly. My mother doesn't say a word, just stares at her. But Mrs. Van Dine isn't done yet. She glances quickly at me, and then at Polly.

"You know as well as I do that there are people who are trying to undermine our American way of life. There are even such people in our very own town. We must keep our guard up. You do understand, don't you?"

"Frankly, Sandy, I don't understand. I don't see how children's costumes could possibly undermine 'our American way of life.' My children—all of them together—were planning to be a Chinese dragon."

I can't be quiet anymore. "It'll be beautiful. We'll make the body out of scraps of fabric—painted all different colors and patterns—and we'll make a head out of papier-mâché—"

"Well, now, there you see what I'm talking about, Mary. There you have it. A Chinese dragon." She leans back in her chair and smiles.

"No, I'm afraid I don't see, Sandy."

"A Chinese dragon. It's a kind of demon, isn't it? Or some kind of protection? Something to keep away evil spirits? I'm not sure. But there is one thing I am sure of. China is a communist country, isn't it? And it was probably their believing in all those godless demons and spirits that left them open to communism. We must keep such ideas away from our children."

"I don't keep any ideas away from my children. I sometimes have to tell them what to do, but I never tell them what to think." My mother sits up straight in her rocking chair; the runners thump hard against the floor.

"Well, I can see that we have very different ideas about how to raise our children."

Mrs. Van Dine's lips are pressed so tightly together you can't even see her lipstick, but then she pastes her little smile back on and says, "I came here today to tell you that I'd like the children of Hillcrest to celebrate a different sort of holiday—a positive, inspiring holiday. I'd like to call it Autumn Fest."

"Autumn Fest." My mother's using her let's-just-forget-you-said-that voice.

"Yes, Autumn Fest. We wouldn't allow any pagan costumes—no ghosts, witches, or vampires. Or any costumes that might frighten the little ones. Some children are terrified of clowns, you know. And, of course, nothing that would encourage dangerous behavior—no acrobats or lion tamers."

"So what's left?" I blurt out.

"Oh, lots of things." Her voice is sticky sweet, the kind of voice some people use when they talk to little kids. "There are all the patriotic costumes—George Washington, Abraham Lincoln, Betsy Ross."

"That sounds an awful lot like the Fourth of July," my mother says.

"Well, of course, you're right. Let's not compete with our glorious Fourth. We really should keep to an autumn theme—pumpkins, scarecrows, things like that."

"You don't think the scarecrows might be too, well, scary?" my mother asks.

"You know, you may be right. I hadn't thought of that. Oh, I see now. You were joking. But I'm sure we can come up with lots of good ideas for costumes."

We. She said *we.* She seems to think she's won my mother over.

"Right now, I'm asking people in town to sign a petition to be presented to the Town Council at their meeting on Monday night."

She reaches for her purse and takes out a folded paper that she opens and hands to my mother. My mother glances at the paper, shakes her head, and hands it back.

"I'm sure you mean well, Sandy, but I can't sign this. I don't think Halloween threatens anyone. I think it's just good fun. And most important, it encourages the kids to use their imaginations."

"Well." Mrs. Van Dine puts the unsigned petition into her purse and clicks it shut. "I believe that unbridled imaginations lead to unbridled behavior. We must train our children to become future citizens, not hooligans."

"I'm not raising hooligans. I'm raising children who think for themselves." My mother's voice could cut through an ice cube.

As Mrs. Van Dine reaches the door, her face is wearing the same perfect smile it's worn almost the whole time since she came in.

"Good-bye, Mary. It was very nice to meet you. And Calliope and Polyhymnia . . ." She seems to be searching for the right words. "Do try to do the right thing. Good-bye."

"Calliope, would you fix Polyhymnia a glass of chocolate milk? I need to go back to the shed and work off some of what I'm feeling right now."

"Sure, Polly, come on."

"Callie, put in lots of chocolate syrup."

"Okay, Polly. Today, I think we could both use some extra chocolate."

What's the matter with me? That Van Dine woman walks in here, looking so perfect, and right away I'm acting like an idiot, even talking like one, worrying what she'll think of me, what she'll think of our house, my mother.

But it was that woman who was the real idiot. She didn't even know when my mother was kidding. "You've been arrested?" Geez, Louise. And all that stuff about paganism and the American way of life. What's more American than Halloween?

So why am I worried about what she thinks? What she'll tell her precious Valeri? Why do I care? I don't care. I don't care what she thinks or what

Valeri thinks or anyone else. Yes, I do. I do care. I care a lot.

As I'm fixing Polly's chocolate milk, I'm thinking that there are two parts of me, like the milk and the syrup. When I pour the syrup into the milk, all the chocolate sinks to the bottom and I have to stir and stir. At first, the chocolate won't budge, won't get mixed into the milk. And then after a while it does.

Callie's Rules:

• If you buy your chocolate milk already made, it saves you a lot of stirring.

5 Free Speech

At dinner, my mother's very quiet. Me, too. I don't feel much like eating tonight. Anyway, it's lentil loaf and pickled tomatoes and kohlrabi salad. I'm not missing much.

Suddenly, Polly bursts out, "Sandy Vandy says we can't be a dragon. She says dragons are too scary."

"Who's Sandy Vandy?" Andy asks.

"I'd better explain," my mother says. Hearing my mother tell the story, it all seems so clear. And it is, for her. She doesn't have to go to school every day with the evil devil Valeri.

Andy looks over at me. "Sorry, Callie. I thought your dragon idea was great. But it looks like it'll just be the younger kids this year."

Andy's always so sure of herself.

"Andy—" My voice catches and I have to stop and start over. "Andy, you're talking as if it's all decided. The Town Council hasn't even met yet. You don't know what they'll decide."

Andy doesn't say anything, just looks down at her plate. She knows I'm right.

My father lowers his glasses. He always perches them on the end of his nose when he's being serious. "Mary," he asks, "what exactly did the petition say?" My father's a lawyer. He's always interested in what he calls "the precise wording of things."

"I don't know exactly what it said," my mother says. "I didn't really read it. After I heard her silly plan, I just glanced at the petition and handed it right back to her."

"Without reading it!"

"Of course without reading it. I didn't need to. She'd already told me what she's planning to do. Why should I read something I wasn't going to sign anyway?"

"Because—" My father nearly shouts the word, then he stops himself and starts again. "Because you can't properly fight a petition if you don't know precisely what it says. I see this all the time. People come into my office who've gotten themselves into deep trouble because they don't bother to read what they're signing."

"But I told you, I didn't sign it."

"Whether you signed it or not is beside the point. She's going to present that petition to the Town Council on Monday night, and we don't know exactly what it says."

"Well, I may not know the exact words, but I do know what it says. Sandy Van Dine wants to ban Halloween, celebrate something she calls Autumn Fest, and make all the children wear costumes that she approves of—nothing 'un-American.'"

My father is quiet for a moment, then he asks, "Van Dine. Is she the wife of Prescott Van Dine, president of the Hillcrest Bank?"

"Probably. Why? What are you thinking?"

"I'm thinking that if the wife of the bank president wants something, she's going to get it. She'll not only have the Town Council supporting her, she'll have the Chamber of Commerce, all the businesspeople in town. The bank holds all their loans and mortgages."

"Well, Herman, you can cave in to that woman—and her bank-president husband—if you want to, but I'm going to fight her."

"And how do you intend to do that?"

"I'm going to go to that Town Council meeting on Monday night and I'm going to have my say."

"Good for you, Mom. It's a matter of free speech. Censorship." Jack sounds like he's getting ready to make a speech. "Yeah, it's censorship. If they start censoring Halloween costumes, what'll be next? The school newspaper?" Jack's a reporter for the high-school paper.

"Actually, Jack"—my father again—"they can censor the school newspaper. Kids don't have the same free-speech rights as adults. But they can't stop us from talking. That *is* a matter of free speech. I'm going to go with you to that meeting, Mary. Anyone else want to join us?"

Everyone starts talking at once, making plans to go to the meeting. I don't say a word. I'm thinking that maybe it would be better if we just let the whole thing pass. Maybe if Mrs. Van Dine doesn't see our whole family there on Monday night, she'll forget about us, forget about our ridiculous house, forget what a mess my mother looked, forget what a fool I made of myself.

Suddenly, I hear my father say, "Well, it looks as though it's settled, then. We're going to the council meeting on Monday night."

Hey, hold on a minute. I didn't hear them ask for a vote, show of hands, or anything. It wouldn't have mattered anyway. Parents decide everything.

Callie's Rules:

- A family is not a democracy.
- Even when your father's a lawyer and talks a lot about rights, it's still not.

That night, I have a terrible nightmare. In my dream, I'm wearing the head of the Chinese dragon, with all my brothers and sisters behind me. We're twisting like a snake, and I've got red, flashing eyes. The streets grow darker and darker, and now I can't see where I'm going. I can't see anything at all. I pull off the dragon's head, and still there's nothing but blackness all around. Behind me, all my brothers and sisters start to scream.

"We've got to keep going," I call to them. "Follow me."

They're all clutching one another, trying to grab me, stumbling and falling. Suddenly, a monk appears. He's holding a candle, but I can't see his face.

"Do you know where we are?" I call out to him. "We've got to get home."

The monk throws back his hood. It's Mrs. Van Dine!

"You can't be a dragon, you little hooligans," she shrieks. "That's un-American!"

From behind me, I hear little Polly start to cry. The monk whirls around, snatches up little Polly, and runs off with her. I try to run after them, but my feet get tangled in something and I can't move. Polly's cries grow fainter.

I wake up shaking and sweating. In the darkness of my room, I'm still seeing Mrs. Van Dine, running off with Polly, still hearing my little sister's cries. I can't make the dream go away.

I stagger into the bathroom. The cold floor tiles shock my feet. I'm awake now, not dreaming, but I still see Polly's frightened face, still hear her crying.

We can't let that woman win. We have to fight her. We have to go to that meeting tomorrow night. When my mother gets up to "have her say," they'll listen to her. My mother can make anyone listen. I know.

6 An Uncharmed Day

In the morning, I'm not so sure. I have the strange feeling you get when you're going up in an elevator and it suddenly stops but your stomach hasn't caught on—it keeps going up. Even while I'm getting dressed, my stomach doesn't come back down.

"Are you okay?" Mel's just pulled her head through her shirt, and she's giving me a funny look. "You just groaned. And you don't look so great."

"I'm okay."

"You sure you're okay? You look kind of sick. Maybe you should stay home from school today."

It would be great to stay home from school. I flop down on my bed. I could stay here all day, read, maybe even have my lunch on a tray.

But staying home won't change anything. I'll have to go to school tomorrow or the next day.

And whenever I do go back to school, Valeri will be waiting for me. She'll be right there.at the front door, smirking at me. In homeroom, she'll whisper about me. She'll stare at me when I change for gym class. And she'll bump into me in the hall, knocking my notebook to the floor so that all the papers go flying.

I'm not even through the door to homeroom when I hear Valeri. She doesn't just have a big mouth, she has a loud one. Loud and piercing. And right now, her loud, piercing voice is knifing me. Or rather my mother.

"She looked just like some kind of hillbilly—overalls, work boots . . ."

I start to shake. If I tried to talk right now, even my voice would shake, so I put on my death stare and walk in. But I'm not staring at Valeri. I'm looking at Wetherly and Raine. Valeri has her back to me. Raine frowns and shakes her head.

"Oh, hi, Callie," Valeri turns and warbles at me, batting her pale, piggy little eyes. Then she sidles over to the far side of the room, her two slaves scurrying after her. Valeri is whispering, and they're all giggling, and every once in a while they shoot a look toward me. Just to make sure I know who they're talking about.

I doodle on the cover of my notebook, as if I don't care. But I do care. My whole life is wrong. I'm wrong.

It's like the charm bracelet. Last year every girl in fifth grade—or at least all the popular ones—had a silver charm bracelet. I could hear the bracelets tinkling on their arms. Before school, in the lunchroom, at recess, the girls used to bend their heads over one another's bracelets and examine each little charm.

They had charms for the sports they played in school—tennis rackets and softballs—and out of school—skis and sailboats and horses. They had charms from the places they'd been; one girl even had a tiny gondola from a trip to Venice. They had charms for their pets and charms for their astrological signs and charms for Christmas and Valentine's Day. The charms were like a special diary, a diary that they shared with each other. But not, of course, with me.

I wanted a charm bracelet more than anything.

I used to imagine myself with a tinkling bracelet on my arm, all the other girls crowding around me, asking to see it. Then I'd take each tiny charm between my fingers and tell what it was for. And we'd all be laughing together.

One day, I went into the jewelry store on Hill-crest Avenue, studied all the silver bracelets in the display case, and picked one out. Maybe I could save up enough to buy it. But when I saw the price on the tiny white tag, I knew I could never save that much. And charms would cost even more. A silver charm bracelet was right up there with horseback riding lessons and trips to Ven-ice: lots more than my parents could afford. But my birthday was coming and I thought, maybe, just once.

I knew it was wrong, but I didn't care. After school, at dinner, at breakfast, I went on about sil-ver charm bracelets. And on my birthday, there was the long gray box. Inside was a silver bracelet, shimmering and delicate, and dangling from it a single charm—a book.

That was it. Just one charm. Not a cluster of them to tinkle when I moved. Not a fascinating glimpse into the fascinating life of a fascinating and popular girl. Just one charm. The wrong charm. A book.

My mother and father were waiting. They looked so pleased. I hugged them and I told them that I was crying because I was so happy. Then I went up to my room and put the bracelet, in its box, on top of my dresser. I never wore it. When my mother asked me why I wasn't wearing the bracelet, I said that we weren't allowed to wear bracelets for gym and I was afraid that if I took it off it might be stolen. But every morning, every night, that long gray box just lay there, screaming at me: *Liar!* So after a while, I put the bracelet in its box away in my top drawer. I couldn't see it anymore, but I knew it was there. Whenever I thought about it, I kind of shriveled up inside.

I still do. And sometimes, when I think about that bracelet, I feel like crying. Like now. But I mustn't. If I cry, Valeri will think it's because of her. Why isn't homeroom starting? What's taking so long?

Alyce! Thank goodness. Alyce is here, and she wants to talk about her roller-skating party. I try to look really interested, but all the while I feel three pairs of eyes on me: Valeri's and Wetherly's and Raine's.

At least in math class there's only Wetherly. And Wetherly is so bad in math that she can't possibly pay attention to me. She sits through the whole class with her face twisted into a tight knot, trying to understand what the teacher is saying. But right after class, she's reverted to her old slimy self.

"Hey, Callie," she says, in a sickening-sweet voice. "Hold on a minute. I really don't understand the homework assignment. You're good in math. Can I come over to your house after school so we can do our homework together?"

"Gee, Wetherly, I'd just be wasting my time. I already did the homework in class."

I put her off this time, and put her down, too, but I know that the little worm will find another way to crawl into my house. Like it's become some sort of tourist attraction:

At the bottom of the hill, on your right, take a look at the purple house. There's a family inside with seven kids. Whole family's freaky. Mother makes these things she calls "weirdos." Father grows pumpkins and sings to them. I'm gonna park the bus right in front here, give you folks a chance to look in through the front window. If you're lucky, you might even get a look at one of them. When you come back to the bus, let me know what you think. After this stop, we're gonna go see the two-headed alligator.

In art, Raine doesn't even wait till class is over. As Mr. Petrocelli is explaining that for the next two weeks we'll be drawing human figures, Raine leans over the table and says in an oily voice, "I know you'll be good at this, Callie. I hear your mother's an *ar*-tist."

This time I don't have a good answer. I just look away.

I meet Alyce for lunch outside the cafeteria. We've just made our way down the line and we're holding our trays, looking for a free table. There don't seem to be two places together anywhere. I finally spot two at the far end of the room, and Alyce and I are heading for them when Valeri comes rushing up.

"Alyce," she says, practically pushing me out of her way. "I have something really important to tell you." And she steers Alyce to her table, where Wetherly and Raine are waiting. There's one empty seat—for Alyce.

The elevator I've been riding all morning turns into a rushing roller coaster. I dump my lunch tray, hurry to the girls' room, lock myself into the farthest stall, and sit down on the edge of the toilet seat to wait for the bell to ring. It's going to be a long wait, lunch period has only just started. I take out *Jane Eyre* and start to read. I'm halfway through the book (and this is the second time I've read it), but I go back to the part where Jane is in a horrible school, and the teacher shames her by making her stand on a high stool.

I know just how Jane felt. I put the book back into my backpack and climb onto the toilet seat. I'm going to stand here, just like Jane, until lunch is over. But when I stand up, my head shows over the top of the door. Why did I have to grow so much over the summer? I crouch down as far as I can, but now I'm bent nearly double and teetering on a very narrow toilet seat. It's all I can do to keep from falling. Jane at least could stand up straight and had her two feet planted on a flat stool.

Isn't lunch over yet? Most days it seems as though I barely have time to eat, but today lunch period is lasting forever. Some girls come into the bathroom, talking, giggling. They're probably posing in front of the mirrors, combing their stupid hair. Why don't they leave? How long does it take to comb their hair? They're not Rapunzel.

Finally, the bell rings and the girls' room empties out. When I step down from the toilet, my legs go all wobbly under me and I can hardly straighten up. I quickly wash my face and put on my best Jane Eyre–defiant look.

Halfway down the hall, Alyce catches up to me. "I'm sorry, Callie. Valeri had to tell me something, and there wasn't any more room at her table."

An anagram for *Alyce K.* is *lackey*, which is what she's become—Valeri's lackey.

I'm not Jane Eyre, I'm Callie Jones. My best

friend is a rat. And all that determination I'd been feeling drains out of me like water down the toilet.

Callie's Rules:

- It's better to stand on a stool than a toilet seat.
- And it's easier to stand on a toilet seat in a bathroom stall if you're short.

7 A Sinister Threat

What was I thinking? I can't go to that Town Council meeting tonight. I can't show up there. Mrs. Van Dine's only seen three of us—boy, did she see us—and I know my mother won't be wearing her working clothes, but still . . . there are nine of us! Even when we just go to the park together, people stare. When we all go in to the council room, they'll stare at us. They'll stare at me. I can't go. I won't go.

None of us should go. Except maybe my father. He's a lawyer; he'll know what to say. And the rest of us can stay home—it's a school night, we shouldn't be out anyway—and afterward he can tell us what happens.

But when I try to talk to my father, he won't budge. "Halloween is for kids," he says. "You kids should be there when we fight this thing."

No matter what I say, I can't change his mind. My father's decided we're all going to that meeting, and that's that. Maybe I should run over to Alyce's house, go down to Mr. Kane's shelter, and lock myself in. There's plenty of food in there, a place to sleep. I could stay until everyone's missing me so much that they've forgotten all about Halloween and they're begging me to come out. But thinking about locking myself in, I remember Jane Eyre, locked into the red room, terrified, screaming to be let out. I probably wouldn't do any better in a bomb shelter, although I could let myself out. But then, what would be the use of locking myself in in the first place?

In a little while, the elevator in my stomach has gone completely crazy, and it's racing up and down and up again nonstop. All afternoon, I pull clothes out of my closet, trying to find a skirt, a sweater, anything like something Valeri Van Dine might just possibly, on a very bad day, wear. I do have one thing that might be okay—a pale blue top and a blue-and-gray-plaid skirt that my grandmother gave me. I get a queasy feeling—I never wrote her a thank-you note. Well, first thing tomorrow, before school, I'll do it. But tonight, thank-you note or not, I have to wear them.

Town Hall isn't far from our house, and it's a warm evening, so we leave the minivan at home and walk there. It's the same way I walk to the library, along Prospect Street. The houses there are beautiful, all white, gleaming in the afternoon sun like a row of sugar cubes. I always try to imagine what it would be like to live in one of those houses. Tonight, the lamps are lit in their front picture windows, but I can't see inside. At every house, they've closed their curtains, and there's only a dim glow that turns the front grass yellow.

The lights are certainly bright in the council chambers, bright enough for everyone to see the nine of us as we walk in. Well, eight of us are walking. My father is carrying Polly. By the time we've made our way to a long bench in the back row, every head in the room has turned around to stare at us. Every head but three in the front row. Two of those heads I recognize: the perfect scoop of chocolate ice cream that sits on Mrs. Van Dine's head and the dirty blonde that Valeri's always tossing. That man sitting next to them, reading a newspaper, must be Mr. Van Dine. The back of his neck is tanned.

The council members are lined up behind a high desk on a platform with flags behind them and name plates in front of them. They start with old business. First, they talk about the town clerk, who's retiring. A million people get up and say what a good job she's done and how it will be impossible to ever replace her. My right leg is itchy. Next is something about finding money in the budget to add more kennels at the animal shelter. After that there's a complaint about a store sign being too big and another one about an illegal fence. Now my left foot is itching. This is all taking a lot of time. Good. Maybe the old business will take so long they won't get to the new business and we can all go home.

No such luck. The chairman—his name plate says he's Mr. Wysnewski—says, "Now, we will address new business. First on the agenda is a petition by Sandra Van Dine, signed by two hundred and fifty certified residents. I believe all the council members have seen the petition. Mrs. Van Dine, would you like to speak?"

Of course she would. Why did he even ask? She walks to the microphone at the front of the room, smiling right and left, and takes hold of the microphone stand. Then she pauses for a few seconds, as though she's waiting for the applause to die down.

"Good evening," she burbles, in the kind of voice you hear only in those commercials for skin cream. "Thank you so much, Mr. Chairman, for giving me this opportunity to speak tonight. I believe most of you know me. Or perhaps you know me best as Mrs. Prescott Van Dine."

She turns to her husband and smiles. This woman could run for queen.

"I've met so many of you at church, worked with you in the Garden Club, the Hillcrest Improvement Association, the Girl Scouts . . . Oh my, I am going on. What I want to say is that you know my work in the community. But perhaps you don't know that I have another job—I'm also a mother."

With a daughter like Valeri, that's nothing to be proud of. She should have stopped with the Girl Scouts.

Now she turns to Valeri and holds out her hand.

Valeri walks over to her mother, takes her hand, and turns to face the audience. They've rehearsed this whole thing!

"If you're a mother, as I am, you know that very soon your children will begin thinking about Halloween, what costumes they're going to wear, how much candy they'll collect. Like all of you, I have very happy memories of Halloween, memories that I would like my children to have as well. But those memories—and it saddens me to say this—belong to an earlier time, a peaceful time, a time when families gathered around the dinner table and held hands to say grace. And I'm sure that many of you—no matter whether you attend a church or a synagogue or a mosque—still do so."

Hey, she forgot about Hindus and Buddhists. Might as well get everybody in.

"I can see from your faces that you can't imagine what Halloween has to do with families and dinner and saying grace. Well, until recently, I couldn't imagine it, either. But a few weeks ago, while I was waiting for a dental appointment, I read an article that shocked me, shocked me deeply. So deeply that I asked if I might take the article home, where I read it over several times. I learned that Halloween is not what we always thought it was.

"What I learned from that article is that Halloween has it roots in pagan celebrations, in godless, devil-worshipping rituals. You look shocked. Well, so was I. But I'd like you to think for a moment, think about some of the costumes the children wear—witch costumes, skeleton costumes, vampire and mummy costumes. Those are the costumes of Satan worshippers."

One or two people start to laugh, but they're the only ones. When they look around and see that everyone else is listening very seriously, they get quiet.

"That did sound funny, didn't it? I know that none of us, no matter what our religion, are Satan worshippers. But that's what Halloween celebrates—satanism. What I just said bears repeating. Halloween is a celebration of satanism. And I ask you, is that what you want to teach your children?"

I can see it now: all those little kids in their witch and ghost costumes, and some guy—wearing animal skins and horns—peers out of a shadowy side yard and waggles his fingers at them. "*Psst*, kids. You in the witch and mummy costumes. Looks like you're ready for a really fun time. Come on over here. I'll teach you some chants, we'll do a few rituals, sacrifice a cat or two, and afterward there'll be candy. Lots of candy." Right, that'll happen.

Mrs. Van Dine's not done yet.

"I recognize so many of you here tonight: Julie Starziano, Bob Fairless, Chris McKenna. I'm sure you want your children to enjoy the holiday. I want my daughter to enjoy it. And even more, I'm hoping that when she grows up, when all our children grow up, they'll have good values. Good, wholesome, God-centered American values. And so tonight I'd like to propose a new celebration for Hillcrest, a celebration we'll call Autumn Fest, with costumes and celebrations appropriate to the season and to the American spirit. I believe that by instituting an Autumn Fest celebration, we will be saying that Hillcrest is a town that stands for American values. Hillcrest can become a model for the entire country."

This is the place where the sound track should kick in with some patriotic country singer wailing about the Yeew-Ess-Aay. Finally, she sits down. Valeri flounces after her. When the chairman asks for discussion, my mother walks to the mike. She's wearing normal clothes tonight. She'll show everyone how silly this whole thing is.

"Mr. Chairman, council members, my name is Mary Jones. I've heard what Sandy Van Dine had to say. In fact, I've heard her twice. I've heard Mrs. Van Dine say that she is concerned about our children. So am I. She believes that we have to guard our children against what she calls inappropriate influences. I agree."

I can't believe what I'm hearing. My mother is standing up there in front of everyone and agreeing with Sandy Van Dine. I feel like I'm in a science-fiction novel, a stranger in an alternate universe.

"Sandy Van Dine wants to be careful of what our children see and hear, what ideas enter their heads. I agree that there are certain things that children, in fact no one, should have to be exposed to. But Halloween, with all its scariness, is not one of those things. Halloween offers our children a chance to let their imaginations run free, for one evening to face their fears and be the scariest creatures they know of, or to become a fictional hero they admire. So I think that rather than banning Halloween, we should encourage it. Thank you."

When my mother comes back to our bench, I can't even look at her. That's it? That's all she had to say? She just doesn't get it. Mrs. Van Dine is practically threatening that Halloween is going to have us kids erecting altars to the devil in our bedrooms and my mother gives a speech about imagination. My father is whispering to her. I can't hear what they're saying, but my father doesn't look happy. He's not as unhappy as I am.

Callie's Rules:

- When someone says you're practically a devil worshipper, it's no good arguing that you're just using your imagination.

A woman, three rows up, is saying something. The chairman interrupts her. "I'm afraid we can't hear you. Would you please come to the microphone?"

"I'm not sure." The woman seems startled to hear her voice coming out of the speakers. "I mean, it's not that I don't agree with what Mrs. Van Dine said. I mean, I do agree with her. About satanism and all. But I just think Halloween is fun. And our kids need a little fun. That's all I have to say."

Mrs. Van Dine is back at the mike. She gives the woman her fake smile and then she says, "I'm sure we all want our children to have fun. But when they celebrate Autumn Fest, they'll be having the right kind of fun. And learning good values as well."

Mrs. Van Dine is hardly back in her seat when my father stands up. This is good. He's a lawyer. He never loses an argument. But now he's signaling for all of us kids to stand up, too. Not just stand up, follow him to the microphone. What is he doing? We won't need a Halloween parade; we've got one right here. And I'm in the middle of it.

When we get to the front of the room, my father lines us all up facing the audience. I move behind Andy and slouch. She's pretty; maybe no one will notice me.

"Mrs. Van Dine," my father says, "wants our children to learn good values. So do we all. I have seven children. . . ."

Why did he have to say that? Everybody can see that there are seven of us, although I was hoping they would only see six.

"I have seven children, and I've tried to teach every one of them good values. My oldest son, Jack, is on the honor roll at school, and he works for the school newspaper."

Okay, point made. Can we all sit down now? Both my legs are itching and so is my nose.

"My oldest daughter, Andy—Andy, would you step forward, please—volunteers at the animal shelter."

Oh, no. Andy's moved over next to my father, and I'm standing up here, out in the open, where everybody can see me. And if he's going to do what I think he's going to do next, I'm doomed.

"My next oldest daughter is Callie."

I'm not itching now, I'm sweating. There's a loud ringing in my ears, and then everything goes black.

This has got to be a nightmare. I'm lying on the floor, with my whole family around me, and some man—wait, I know him, he's Dr. Fritz, our family doctor—Dr. Fritz is holding my wrist and saying something to my mother. I can't quite hear him yet. Now I can; he's saying I'll be all right, only fainted, growth spurt, not enough blood to the brain.

If this is a nightmare, why can't I wake up? My father is kneeling down, picking me up in his arms, and carrying me out of the room. I see the lights, the flags, as we go past. It's the council chamber! I've fainted in the council chamber! In front of everyone—the entire Town Council, Mrs. Van Dine, Valeri. Practically the whole town.

Now I'm lying on a bench in the hallway, and my mother is propping me up, handing me a paper cup of water, and saying that she wants me to stay home from school tomorrow. As if I could ever go to school again.

8 A Committee and a Chairman

This day is really working out well: staying in bed, no school, my meals on a tray. Until my father comes home with the paper. There's a report on last night's town meeting.

"You can skip this first part," he says. "We were there. Read the rest."

My hands are shaking so badly I can hardly hold the paper. Did they report that one Miss Calliope Jones, eleven years old, of 3 Potter Place, Hillcrest, fainted in the middle of the meeting? Fainted flat on the floor and had to be carried out like a dead person?

No, they skipped that part. Guess I'm not very important, even when I faint. I read the article from the place where my father is pointing.

In additional comments, Dr. Fritz Jack-enthaler noted that the petition had been signed by most of the medical profession-als in Hillcrest and that they would like to suggest the committee's guidelines indicate that, rather than candy, appropriate treats would be healthy alternatives such as apples and toothbrushes.

Hiram Steadman, the owner of Stead-man's Hardware, in a related point, com-mented that the painting of store windows by schoolchildren blocks his displays and can be detrimental to his business. He added that window painting was, in his words, "a pure waste of a perfectly good school day. Those kids ought to be in school learning something."

Finally, Mrs. Van Dine suggested that a committee, comprised of community leaders, clergymen, doctors, and child psychologists, be formed to study the various issues raised: replacing the town's Halloween parade with an Autumn Fest celebration, suggesting appropriate treats, and discontinuing the tradition of painting store windows. The Town Council agreed and invited Mr. Prescott Van Dine, president of the Hillcrest Bank, to chair the committee. The committee will report its findings at the next council meeting, in two weeks.

There was no further business, and the meeting was adjourned.

Why form a committee? Why even wait two weeks? People like the Van Dines don't need committees; they don't even need a Town Council. They just decide what they want and they get it.

Callie's Rules:

- One good thing about being someone other people don't pay attention to: when you do something really, really embarrassing, the newspaper doesn't pay any attention, either.

9 The Majority Wins

One day in bed, that's all I get. You'd think fainting in front of the whole Town Council would earn me at least two, but no, my mother says I'm fine and I have to go back to school today.

Maybe I could have a disease, a really bad disease. Typhus, like what Jane Eyre's friend Helen Burns died of. But no. I'm pretty sure typhus was one of the things I got shots for when I was a baby. I've probably been inoculated against all the really deadly stuff, and for anything less my mother would say I wasn't going to die and would haul me out of bed and send me to school.

But there's more than one way to die. And one of them is named Valeri. After my dramatic scene, Valeri's going to make my life more miserable than it's ever been. It looks like I'll be spending every lunch period for the rest of the year in the girls' room.

This morning I'm so angry at my mother, I can't even look at her. I stomp down the stairs, snatch my books from the hall table, and slam the front door behind me. My mother is at the door before I've even reached the curb.

"Calliope, you can't go to school without breakfast."

"Don't tell me what I can't do."

"Hold on there, young lady."

My mother catches me by the shoulders and whirls me around to face her. She's still wearing her pajamas. Geez, Louise. Does she know what she looks like?

"If you're angry at me, say so."

"Okay, I'm mad at you. Can I go now? You told me I have to go to school today. You sure wouldn't want me to be late."

"Not yet. Tell me why you're angry at me."

"I'm angry at you because you didn't say anything."

"When?"

"At the council meeting."

"I thought I did."

"Not enough. You didn't say enough. Nobody even listened to you. Didn't you read the paper? It's as good as decided. Halloween's finished."

And not just Halloween. I'm finished, too.

"I see. Well, then, miss, if you think you can do better, why don't you speak at the next Town Council meeting?"

"Okay, then. I will!"

What kind of a mess have I gotten myself into now? I can't speak at the town meeting. Go up to the front of the room, stand at the mike, with all those people looking at me? Even Valeri and Mrs. Van Dine. I can't do it. But now I have to. My mother dared me, and I took the dare. I've got to do it.

Callie's Rules:

- Mothers don't have to tell you to do something you don't want to do. They make you say it yourself.

Maybe I should just turn around, go back home, tell my mother I was wrong, and can't we forget the whole thing. No, I won't do that. It might work with someone like Alyce's mother, but not mine. She'll say something about it being a matter of principle, that I have to learn to stand up for the things I believe in—all her usual speeches. And then she'll get my father to agree with her.

I feel like I'm in some weird game of dodgeball: I'm not on any team; I'm in the middle, and both sides are trying to get me. On one side there's my mother and father, and on the other there's Valeri.

And here she comes now. She's trying to look all serious and sympathetic, but I know the minute she turns her back she'll be smirking and running to tell everyone.

"Callie, are you all right? You had us all so worried Monday night. And you weren't in school yesterday. What's wrong with you?"

"Valeri," I say, using a shaky voice and making my face really tragic, "I don't know yet. No one will tell me."

For the first time in her life, Valeri is speechless. That serious look on her face is for real now.

Hooray for me! Valeri threw a ball at me, and I dodged it. But I still have that speech to make. All through homeroom, English, math, I try to come up with something to say. My ideas sound good in my head, but when I write them down and read them back, they're awful. The first thing I write makes me sound like a whiny little kid. The next one is just angry. The third one makes no sense at all; I have some kind of good idea in the beginning, but when I read it over, it just seems silly.

It's the last class of the day. I'm getting really mad at myself, and I push down so hard on my pencil, I break the point. When I reach down to get another out of my purse, my speech blows onto the floor. And suddenly, planted on my dreadful speech is a sneaker, a white sock, and a frayed jeans leg—Shane Belcher's sneaker, sock, and jeans. He grabs the paper and puts it on his desk.

I try to snatch it back, but Shane is two seats behind and my arm is shorter than his leg. Besides, he's already started reading it.

"What's this for, Cal?" he whispers, screwing his eyebrows together.

Cal. My chest starts to quiver. Not Calliope. Not Callie. Cal. Every part of my brain tells me I should say it's none of his business, but I keep hearing Shane saying "Cal." I twist around in my seat and whisper back, "I can't tell you now. I'll explain after class."

"Calliope, Shane." The teacher's voice rings through the room. "Is there something you two would like to share with the rest of the class?"

Twenty-five heads turn and twenty-five pairs of eyes are staring at us. Can this day get any worse?

When the bell rings, I try to hurry out ahead of Shane. But he catches up with me at the door. And he's still got my miserable speech.

"Give that back to me, Shane. It's mine."

"I will, Cal, just as soon as you tell me what this is all about."

He called me Cal again. And before I know what I'm doing, I'm heading to our next class with Shane and telling him the whole story.

"The Van Dines," he says, "think they own this town. What we need is a petition of our own."

Of course! A petition! I'll get the kids in town to sign a petition to keep Halloween. It'll be like a vote. If I get more signatures than that woman's 250, then we'll win.

I'm walking away when I remember. Shane said

we. He said, "*We* need a petition of our own." I hurry back.

"Shane, would you like to help me write it? The petition, I mean."

"Sure, I'll come now."

I've done it again—opened my big, fat, stupid mouth. That's how this whole thing started in the first place, when I blurted out to Mrs. Van Dine that my mother was home. Or this morning, when I got mad at my mother and said I'd speak at the Town Council meeting. I never learn.

Callie's Rules:

• Monks have the right idea. If you never open your mouth, you get into a lot less trouble.

And now Shane is standing there, looking at me, expecting me to take him to my house. Well, I might as well get it over with. He won't have to see my mother; she'll be working in the shed. We can just sit on the front steps and not even go into the house. Maybe no one will see that we're walking home together. Maybe.

10 Everything Proper and Legal

"Hey, isn't this the house that has the robots in front for Halloween? Those robots are great!"

"We call them weirdos."

"That's a good name for them. When I was a kid, I always saved this house for last. You live around here?"

"Right here. This is my house."

"You're the people with the weirdos? Wow! Where do you get them?"

"My mother makes them. She's a sculptor. She makes a new weirdo every year, and she's just started the one for this year. It doesn't have a name yet; she just calls it Number Eighteen."

What's the matter with me? It's like when I start talking, I can't stop. I open my mouth and words come spilling out—like I have a leak in my brain.

"Can I see it?"

What do I do now? Half of me, the milk-on-top-of-the-glass part, is thinking, Just tell him that your mother doesn't like anyone to see a weirdo until she's finished, or that she doesn't like anyone walking in while she's working. But the chocolate-on-the-bottom-of-the-glass part is thinking it'll be okay, that Shane'll be okay.

Shane is looking at me, waiting for an answer. His hair kind of sticks up in little spikes.

"Wait, there's one thing I'd better warn you about. When we go into the shed, don't let Polly out of her cage."

"Polly? What is she? A parrot?"

"No, she's my sister."

"Your sister. In a cage. You're kidding, right?"

"No, I'm not kidding. It's the truth. Polly's my sister, and she's in there in a cage. Do you want to go in? Or are you too chicken?"

"I'm not chicken!"

"Well, come on then."

I lead the way to the shed, but at the door, I stop and say, "You're sure you want to go in? You can still turn around and go home."

"I said I'm going in and I am."

Shane's face gets all red, and he looks like he could punch someone.

"Okay, then. It's your choice."

I open the shed door, and Shane follows me in.

"There she is. There's Polly."

I stoop down and kiss the top of her fuzzy head.

"You should have seen your face, Shane. We call it her cage, but it's really a giant playpen. We keep Polly in it because there's metal and shears and solder all over the place. It's not safe to let her out. So she stays in there with her toys, and my mother can keep an eye on her while she works. You really should have seen your face."

"Calliope, you've brought a friend home." My mother's not wearing her welder's mask today, and her voice sounds normal.

"Hi, Mom. This is Shane. We're going to work on something for school." I don't want to tell my mother about the petition. Not yet. I'm still mad at her.

"Hello, Shane. I see you're looking at the weirdos."

"Hey, I remember this one—it blows smoke out

of its ears. And this one over here—its teeth rattle. When I was little, I thought there were people inside, sort of like knights in suits of armor, making them do those things. These are great, Mrs. Jones. And you think them all up yourself?"

"Actually, I don't think them up. They think themselves up. I start cutting out pieces, without any idea of what I'm doing, and after a while they tell me what they want to become. Calliope, why don't you fix a snack for yourself and Shane?"

No one's in the house. The younger kids won't get home from school for another hour, Jack's at his job, and I guess Andy's gone to a friend's house. That's good. I'm not ready to tell anyone yet about the petition.

I give Shane a peanut butter sandwich and go to get some paper and a couple of pencils. By the time I come back, Shane's already finished the sandwich.

"Okay, let's get started. This is how we should begin."

At the top of the paper, I write: *We the undersigned children residing in the town of Hillcrest . . .*

"We have to start that way," I explain to Shane.

"My father's a lawyer and a lot of his documents start like that."

"Okay," Shane says, and he pulls the paper in front of him and writes *being of sound mind.*

"Hah! Very funny. But we have to be serious."

"Well, it sounds like you're writing a last will and testament."

"Have you got a better idea?"

"No. Okay. We'll do it your way. Could I have another sandwich? I don't think so good when I'm hungry."

We've got the petition mostly written, but Shane's looking hungry again.

"Sorry, Shane. We're out of peanut butter." He reaches for an apple. Shane has astoundingly long arms. All the while he's crunching, I keep writing.

"Okay, Shane, we're done. You take it home, type it up, and print it out. And don't forget to make lines for the names. Maybe make a border of stars so it'll look patriotic."

Shane is about to grab another apple when I pull the bowl away.

"We're saving these for our school lunches tomorrow."

Shane's still looking hungry when he heads for home.

Callie's Rules:

- If you want a boy to leave, cut off his food supply.

11 Grown-Ups Always Say No

Yesterday, the petition seemed like a brilliant idea. This morning I'm not so sure. What if nobody wants to sign it? I'm not a kid who starts things at school, I'm not a kid other kids listen to.

Shane's not in homeroom yet. Maybe he didn't print out the petition. Nobody knows but Shane, and if he hasn't done it yet, I can just tell him to forget the whole thing. But no such luck. There he is. He comes right over to where I'm standing and starts handing me some petitions. Valeri's staring at us, with her little piggy eyes. Let her stare. Jane Eyre wasn't afraid of anyone staring at her. I walk over to Maxine and Madeline, holding a petition.

"They want to change Halloween. The Town Council. They want to stop Halloween and have something called Autumn Fest. We won't be allowed to wear the costumes we want. We'll have to be pumpkins or George Washington and crummy stuff like that. They might not even let us paint the store windows. We made up a petition, Shane and I."

The kids like Shane. Maybe if they know he helped write the petition, they'll want to sign.

"I don't get it, Callie," Maxine says. "What are you talking about?"

Okay, Callie, take a deep breath and start over.

"Last Monday night, Valeri's mom presented a petition at the Town Council meeting."

Valeri's not the only one listening now.

"They want to take away all our fun on Halloween. In fact, it won't even be called Halloween anymore. It will be something called Autumn Fest. And we won't be able to decide what costumes we can wear. They won't let us wear anything scary—no vampires or witches. I had this idea for a Chinese dragon costume. Now we won't be allowed to do that. We'll all have to wear stupid costumes with what Valeri's mom called 'an autumn theme.' Some people are even saying that we shouldn't trick-or-treat for candy. We should get apples and pencils and stuff like that."

"Go ahead, Cal," Shane says. "Tell them about the petition."

"Mrs. Van Dine got two hundred and fifty people to sign her petition. If we can get more kids to sign ours, mine and Shane's, we'll win. The Town Council will have to let us keep Halloween the way it's always been."

Valeri elbows her way through the kids.

"Callie," she says, "you're making a big mistake. You don't think your pathetic little petition is going to matter, do you? There's already a committee—my father's the chairman—and they're going to arrange everything. Go ahead, Callie, start your petition; it won't make any difference."

"It will if I get enough kids to sign."

Valeri starts to smile.

"What's so funny, Valeri?"

"You are, Callie. You can pass around your little piece of paper, but you won't get any of the popular kids to sign it."

Valeri's right about that. No popular kid is going to sign anything of mine. I couldn't even ask them to write in my autograph album when we left fifth grade. I'm thinking about giving up, when I remember something.

Callie's Rules:

- There are always a lot more unpopular kids than popular ones.
- That's the way the popular kids feel they're special.

So the popular kids won't sign. But I can try to get all the others.

By the time Mrs. Thigpen walks in the door, a lot of kids have signed. Some of the kids who didn't get a chance say they'll sign after class. The day keeps getting better. Between classes, kids find me and ask to sign the petition—kids I don't even know. I'm flying. Until lunch, when two things happen. First, it's Alyce.

"Callie," she says, and she can't even look at me, "I want to take my name off your petition."

"Why? You signed it this morning."

"I know, but now I don't think it's such a good idea."

"It's Valeri, isn't it? She got to you."

"No, it's not Valeri." Alyce looks panicked. "It's . . . it's my father. He'd be really mad if he knew I had signed something like that."

"Like what? Something like what?"

"Something that goes against the town, that's what. You can get into real trouble, Callie."

Then the second thing happens. Valeri flounces over and tells Alyce that they've saved a place for her at their table. Fine, let her go. I'm never going to speak to Alyce again anyway. But before she leaves, Valeri looks at me with a funny smile on her face, and she says, "Callie, I want to ask you something."

Here it comes.

"Is Shane your boyfriend?"

I just look at her for maybe half a minute, a look that says I think she must be crazy. "No," I say, "he isn't."

This time I did something right. I didn't act embarrassed or silly or anything. I just said no. Just that: "No, he isn't." I know what Valeri was hoping I would say. She wanted me to say that Shane *was* my boyfriend. That would have been good for a laugh—a nerd like Callie with a boyfriend. Or maybe she thought I'd act all flustered, as if I really liked Shane and wished he *could* be my boyfriend. Either way, she'd have it all over school by tomorrow. But for what was probably the first time in my life, I didn't go and make a fool of myself. I simply said, "No, he isn't." Good for you, Cal.

Or maybe not so good. The first thing I ever manage to do right is not doing something, actually not saying something. Maybe I should stick to that from now on—make it a rule.

Callie's Rules:

- If you want to stay out of trouble, take a vow of silence.

By the end of the day, I've got thirty-five signatures, and Shane has forty-two. We're going to need a lot more than seventy-seven if we're going to win. So after school, even though I always walk home, I wait at the bus lines. I'm giving the kids my speech when the principal, Mr. Nolan, slinks up.

"What is your name, miss?"

"Calliope Jones."

"Miss Jones, may I see that piece of paper you're holding?"

"It's only a petition, Mr. Nolan. I'm not doing anything wrong."

"Yes, Calliope, you are. You are disrupting one of the bus lines and keeping the driver waiting. Now give me that piece of paper."

As he reads it, his face turns all dark. "Calliope, I cannot permit you to circulate this petition on school grounds. What you are proposing—in what you choose to call a petition—is defying authority."

And he tears up my petition! Everyone in school—well, not everyone, only the kids—call him Mr. No-Man. Jack and Andy warned me. They said, whatever you ask for, he'll say no. If you want to use the secretary's telephone, he'll say no. If he lets one person use it, he'll have to let everyone in the school use it. If you forget your homework and want to run home to get it, he'll say no. He'll say, "Let this be a lesson to you. Before you leave home, check that you have everything you need."

Once Jack wanted to start a Young Democrats Club, and Mr. Nolan said no. He said, "If we allow one club like that, we'll have to allow a club for every political view. Before you know it, we'd have a Young Socialists Club or even a Young Anarchists Club. No, I can't allow it." And when the eighth grade wanted to raise money for a trip to Washington, Mr. Nolan had gone on and on about insurance and liability and teachers' contracts. Of course, he'd said no.

So here I am, standing in the middle of the bus line, watching Mr. No-Man stuffing my precious petition into his pocket and slithering off. What do I do now? I've lost a whole page of signatures, and even with Shane's we still won't have enough. And now I can't collect any more at school.

Then it hits me. Hillcrest Middle School isn't the only school in town. It's not even the only place to find kids. There's the high school and the elementary schools. There's the library. And Cubby's. I can do it. I can march right into Cubby's and ask the kids to sign. Just not today. I'll do it tomorrow.

Jack says he'll help. He's still mad about the Young Democrats Club, and he starts going on about how they can't stifle free speech. I don't wait for him to finish. I hand him some petitions and go to find Andy.

"Oh, that Mr. No-Man," she groans. "Remember my Girl Scout project? When I wanted to bring in the animals from the animal shelter to get them adopted? And he said no. Of course. 'Those animals might be diseased.'" Andy sounds exactly like Mr. Nolan. "'Or what if a student is bitten? No, Andromeda, you may not bring animals into this school building or onto the grounds.' Give me lots of copies of your petition, Callie. I'll get them signed for you."

Even Mel says she'd get some of the kids at the elementary school to sign.

12 Fateful Friday

It's Fundamentals Fridays again, the dread day of test preparation. Mrs. Thigpen is handing out worksheets, but when she gets to my desk, she stops and says, "Calliope, I'd like to speak to you. Please wait at my desk."

What now? Did Mr. No-Man report me? Is this petition stuff going to go in my permanent record? Why make me go and stand in front of her desk? Mrs. Thigpen can do it right now—announce in her foghorn voice that Calliope Jones must report to the principal's office.

Even without the announcement, everyone's staring me. Can they hear my bones clattering?

"Calliope, please take a seat."

Oh boy, this is going to be even worse than I thought. In the movies, when they ask someone to sit down first, it means they've got some really terrible news. Like someone died.

"Calliope, since there would be no point in your continuing with the pretests, I've been trying to think what would be a better use of your time. I've been teaching for thirty years, Calliope, and I've become a fairly good judge of student abilities. You read a good deal, don't you?"

I'm really confused now. I nod.

"Because while it's true that grammar and sentence structure, punctuation and spelling can all be taught, only a student who reads—and who reads a great deal—could have completed the pretests as quickly and as well as you have done. What have you been reading in class, Calliope?"

"*Lorna Doone*. The class is reading *Lorna Doone*." I didn't exactly lie. I didn't say I'd been reading it; I said the class was reading it.

"I didn't ask what the class is reading. I asked what *you've* been reading in class every day."

I'm finished. School's hardly begun, and I'm not only in trouble with Mr. Nolan, I'm in bigger trouble with Mrs. Thigpen.

"I've been listening, Mrs. Thigpen. Really, I

have. I've heard every word you've said."

"Be that as it may, you haven't answered my question. What have you been reading?"

"*Jane Eyre.*" My voice comes out as a whisper.

"*Jane Eyre.* That was—still is—a great favorite of mine. I love all the characters. Each one is so vivid. Although I do think they tend to make overly long speeches."

"Oh, I know. Sometimes I skip over the really long ones." Why did I say that? Now I'll probably get some kind of lecture on the value of reading every word: *After all, Calliope, how can you know what the author intends if you don't read every word?*

"I must confess," Mrs. Thigpen says, and she's smiling, "that I do, too. Sometimes. But let me tell you what I've planned for you, Calliope. Since you won't be preparing for the state tests, I'd like you to do some original writing for me."

"Like a book report? I could do one on *Jane Eyre.*"

"A book report is not precisely what I had in mind. I'm sure you've done a great many book reports in school. No, what I'd like you to write is something completely your own—a short story, a collection of poems, an extended essay. Even a play. Do you think you can do that?"

I'm not sure. I've written a lot of stories and poems, but they're just for me. They're private. I don't show them to anyone. Mrs. Thigpen will read what I write. And she's going to give me a grade on it.

"I could do two book reports. One on *Jane Eyre* and one on *Lorna Doone.*" She's got to like that idea. I kind of like it, too, even if I do have to read that boring book.

"No, Calliope, you can't get around me that easily. I want a piece of original writing from you. You can decide what form it will take, but it can't be a book report."

For the rest of the period, all the other kids are sitting at their desks, bent over their worksheets, writing, erasing, writing again. And I'm sitting at my desk, with a pencil and a piece of paper, and my mind is as blank as that paper.

Callie's Rules:

• Teachers are just like the popular kids.

They make the rules and you have to follow them.

Just as the bell is ringing, Mrs. Thigpen announces, "Remember, class, there'll be a test on Monday. Make sure you're prepared."

A test? On Monday? I must not have been listening when Mrs. T talked about it. Well, it doesn't matter. I always do great on tests. I've just got to remember to take my time and not finish before everybody else. What I've really got to worry about for Monday is that Town Council meeting.

13 A Test Case

"Please clear your desks, class, of everything but pens and pencils. I'll be passing out paper."

Why do teachers love to give tests on Monday? Is it so we'll worry about it all weekend? Just judging from some of the kids' faces, that plan seems to be working. Not me, though. I've got a lot more important things to worry about than some stupid grammar test.

"Now, class, I know that *Lorna Doone* is a difficult book to read, and for that reason, I've tried to help you through the first two chapters. We've been discussing the period and the setting; I've explained some of the archaic language and dialect. But now I want you to probe beneath the surface of the book."

Hold on a minute! *Lorna Doone*? This is a test

on *Lorna Doone*? But I never even got past the first paragraph. How am I going to take this test? This is so unfair. Why do they decide that we have to read a really boring book? And take a test on it?

Uh-oh. She's writing the questions on the board. There are two of them, and she says to choose one.

1. How was schooling in seventeenth-century England like or different from education in twenty-first-century America?
2. How was the behavior of boys in that same place and time like or different from that of boys in the present day?

"I want you to think through your answer before you begin writing. Plan what you want to say and use examples from the book to illustrate your answer."

Mrs. T knew that I was reading *Jane Eyre*; she thought that was great. I didn't think I had to read *Lorna Doone*. What do I do now? Wait a second, just hold on, Callie. Don't panic. What was that first question again? Schooling . . . in England . . . in the seventeenth century. There's a whole lot in

Jane Eyre about her school. Okay, it was the nineteenth century, not the seventeenth, but still, it was in England. How different could it be? I can answer that question. I can do it.

I scribble down some notes—the ideas are coming to me really fast—and pretty soon I'm ready to start writing.

> *English schools in the seventeenth century would have seemed very strange to an American student today, but in some ways they were not very different. One of the major differences is that four hundred years ago, children had to pay to go to school. Poor children were considered charity cases and were looked down on.*

I'd like to say something here about how some kids are still looked down on—like me, for instance. But I won't.

> *The school poor children attended was not called a school, but an institution. Today, public education is free for everyone.*

Girls at that time also had to wear uni-
forms to school. Today, only students in
parochial schools and a few public schools
wear uniforms.

Uniforms would be an improvement. At least then I wouldn't have to spend so much time figuring out what's the right thing to wear—and getting it wrong anyway.

They also lived at the school and slept
two to a bed. Some students today do live
at schools, called boarding schools, but I'm
fairly certain they each have their own beds.
They ate their meals at long tables and
the food was quite terrible. That's not so dif-
ferent from what we call the school cafeteria,
where the food is also poor. However, at that
time, the girls were given coffee with each
meal, whereas now our parents say that cof-
fee will stunt our growth.

Maybe I should cross out that last part. It's not really about education. But Mrs. T wanted us to put in illustrations, and it will make my answer longer. And she'll love the "whereas"—my father always says that.

In other respects, education then was similar to education today. The girls studied some of the same subjects, like history.

But now we've got four hundred more years of history to study.

And bells were rung all day long to indicate when the girls were to change to another subject or when it was time for a meal.

But a major difference was the way the girls were punished. When a girl broke a rule, she could be beaten with a switch made of twigs, or made to stand on a stool in the middle of the classroom. Today, we get sent to the principal's office.

That can be humiliating, but at least we don't get hit. Although I have heard that in parochial schools, students still do get their knuckles rapped.

But one of the biggest differences was
that the physical conditions

"Physical conditions"—Mrs. T will like that.

at the school were so harsh. The rooms were
freezing cold, and the girls were kept half-
starved. The idea was that their souls would
benefit from suffering and privation.

Good words. She'll like those, too.

They worried a lot about the girls' souls.
They had to pray in the morning and before
every meal, and sing hymns. Today, we don't
have to pray in school, because that violates
the separation of church and state.

I know Mrs. Thigpen will be very impressed by
that last part.

"Time is up, class. Please make sure your name
is on every page of your papers and pass them forward."

Wait a second, I'm not finished. I have to write

some sort of conclusion, a really strong last sentence. No chance of that now. But I'm sure Mrs. Thigpen will really like what I wrote.

Callie's Rules:

- My father always says, "When you don't know how to do something, try to use what you do know."
- Listen to your father. The things he tells you might be useful some time.

14 Kids Don't Get a Vote

Well, conclusion or not, I don't have time to think about Mrs. Thigpen's test. The town meeting's coming up, and there's still a lot of work to do. Every night, I add up the numbers of signatures everybody's gotten. By Friday evening, there are 257 names, seven more than Mrs. Van Dine's. We're going to win! It's a simple question of democracy. The one with the most votes wins, and we have the most votes. I feel as if I ought to be marching at the head of the Fourth of July parade, wearing red, white, and blue and twirling a baton.

On Monday night, when we all file into the council chambers, I go first, leading the way past the Van Dines, who are sitting in the front row to the left of the aisle, and over into the first row on the right. There aren't nine seats in the row, so some of us have to take seats behind. A few minutes later, Shane Belcher walks in. He keeps his head down, not looking at me, and heads toward the back. He's wearing a button-down shirt and he's slicked his hair down, although one spike got loose and is sticking up.

Tonight, I'm too excited to pay any attention to the old business. It seems like forever until the chairman says, "Before we hear the committee's report in response to Mrs. Van Dine's petition, is there any further discussion?"

My hand shakes when I raise it.

"May I speak, please?"

My knees are shaking even worse when I walk to the microphone and the petitions in my hand are fluttering like leaves in a storm. *Don't faint, Callie. You can't faint. Not now. Not again.*

"For the record, miss, would you state your name."

"Calliope Jones."

"Miss Jones, how old are you?"

I'm confused. Why is he asking how old I am?

"I'm eleven."

"I'm sorry, Miss Jones, but only legal residents

of the town may speak at these meetings."

"But I am a legal resident. I was born here. I've lived here all my life. Except some summers when I go and stay with my grandparents."

Stupid, stupid, stupid. Why did I have to go and say that?

"I'm afraid I didn't make myself clear. To be a legal resident, you must pay property taxes in this town."

Now my father is standing next to me, and he's put a hand on my shoulder.

"My name is Herman Jones, and I am a legal resident of Hillcrest."

"Would you like to speak, Mr. Jones?"

"Yes, I would. And I'd like to do more than speak. I'd like to present, for the council's consideration, an opposing petition, a petition that has been signed by two hundred fifty-seven individuals."

"Are all of those two hundred fifty-seven individuals taxpayers in this town?"

My father looks down at me. I shake my head.

"No? Then we'll proceed."

I can't believe this. There's my father, looking as if he's standing in front of the principal's desk.

My father. The regular parent. The one who leaves the house every morning for the train, with all the other fathers, works in an office, like all the other fathers, wears a suit and tie. My father, the lawyer who knows all about legal things. As we walk back to our seats, I feel as though I'm standing on the beach and a big wave has just washed over my feet, pulling the sand out from under me. I should have stayed fainted the first time.

"Well, then," the chairman is saying, "if there's no further discussion, let's proceed. As you probably recall, at the last meeting it was suggested that we form a committee to study the matter of the Halloween celebration. Mr. Van Dine took the chairmanship of the committee, which consisted of a number of clergymen, teachers, a child development expert, and several parents. First, let me say, Mr. Van Dine, that we all know what a busy man you are and we are most grateful that you so kindly took on this responsibility. So, without further ado, I will give the floor to Mr. Van Dine."

Oh, no. This isn't over. Why didn't we leave before, when the chairman wouldn't even look at my petition?

"Thank you, Mr. Chairman. I believe you have a copy of our final report. That report summarizes the committee's work and our conclusions. But I believe some members of the committee would like to add some comments of their own. Matthew?"

"Thank you, Mr. Van Dine. My name is Matthew Volkenrath. Our committee did a lot of studying about this thing. And what I learned just shocked me. Really shocked me. If it were up to me, I'd shut Halloween down. Not just in Hillcrest—everywhere.

"You may think Halloween is just kid stuff, just fun, but it's certainly not. We learned . . . Well, for instance, witch costumes. You probably don't know that those are what the Druids wore when they were practicing human sacrifice. That's right. You heard me. Human sacrifice. When our kids dress up that way, they're reenacting satanic rituals. Let me give you a little history here."

Matthew Volkenrath pulls out a sheet of paper and looks it over.

"I just told you about the Druids. Well, this goes back more than two thousand years. The Druids had a celebration, on November first, where they honored the god of the dead. They believed that the night before—this was October thirty-first— the spirits of the dead came back to visit the living. And if living people didn't give food to the dead spirits, all kinds of terrible things would happen.

"Remind you of anything? That's right—trick or treat. Give us food or we'll do terrible things to you. Pretty sickening stuff. But that's not all. Those jack-o'-lanterns you carve? Well, those were meant to scare off ghosts, goblins, witches, and all those spirits that were roaming around on the night of the dead. Black cats, they're kept by witches and satanists. Bats and owls? They're supposed to be able to communicate with the dead. You had no idea, did you? And, of course, I don't have to explain skeletons, skulls, and corpses.

"So what's wrong with Halloween? Everything. I'm like you. I had no idea before we started look- ing into this. But now that I know . . . Well, as I said, I'd just as soon do away with the whole thing. It's just satanism; that's all it is."

I can't believe what I'm hearing. According to him, we're all of us, every kid in town, even my family, devil worshippers. This has got to be a joke, some kind of Halloween prank. Why is no one laughing?

Now a woman is coming to the mike.

"Good evening. My name is Pat Kinderly, and I'm a child psychologist. I know this is a weeknight, so I'll get right to the point.

"You're probably thinking that what Matt has just been telling you is all history, all in the past, that Halloween has now become just a harmless and fun activity. I'm afraid that is not the case. Across the country, police departments report increases in vandalism and destruction of property on Halloween night. Now, I know our children aren't vandals, they're not hooligans. They just want to dress up in costumes and go out collecting candy. Yes, but what are we teaching them when even little toddlers, who can barely speak, know how to say, 'Trick or treat'?

"Do you see what I'm seeing? All those innocent, sweet-faced children, scurrying from door to door, smiling, laughing, trick-or-treat bags in their plump, little hands, and practicing extortion. Not a pretty picture, is it?

"Well, look, I think I've said enough. I've left

several published studies in the council office. If you'd like to know more—and I think you should—stop in and have a look at them."

What's this all about? First, we kids were all going to become devil worshippers, and now, we'll all grow up to hide switchblades in our leather jackets.

A lot of people are standing up to speak. They're forming a line in the aisle, and waiting for the microphone. It seems like half the room has something to say.

"Look, I'm no child psychologist, I'm just a father. But, you know, I remember when I was a kid that Halloween was one of the most fun times of the year. I kind of want my kids to have that same kind of fun."

Now they're not even waiting for the mike, or even standing up, just calling out their comments.

". . . I agree . . ."

". . . comic books are fun, too. What's fun isn't necessarily what's good for them."

". . . candy. What's so bad about candy? Not all the time, but once in a while . . ."

"Like an occasional drink for a grown-up."

". . . grown-ups, not kids . . ."

The arguments are bouncing back and forth like tennis balls.

". . . making too big a deal out of this . . ."

". . . too scary for kids. Some of those costumes terrified my little girl."

"Fairy tales are scary, too. Should we ban them?"

"Yes, all those evil queens and wicked step-mothers. I banned them from our house. I don't even want them in the library."

Now the chairman is banging his gavel on the table. "Let's have some order here, please. Quiet down. Now, the council has read the committee's reports, and some of us have also taken a look at the articles Ms. Kinderly left for us. And, of course, we've been listening to all the comments you people have made here tonight. We think we know everything we need to know, and we're ready to make our decision. So if you will give us just a few minutes, the council will confer, and then we'll let you know what we've decided."

The council members all bend their heads toward the chairman, who has his hand over his mike so we can't hear what he's saying. I don't need to hear what he's saying. The council members don't, either. They're all nodding their heads. They don't even take a few minutes. It's more like a few seconds. They all sit back in their seats; the chairman takes his hand away from the mike and bangs his gavel again.

"The council members have talked this all over, and all of us think that, on balance, yes, Halloween's fun for kids, but Autumn Fest will be fun, too. Even more importantly, there are certain very unpleasant, even frightening things about Halloween, and there's nothing of the sort associated with an Autumn Fest. So as the council sees it, there's no good reason not to give Autumn Fest a try. We took a vote, and we all decided in favor of replacing Halloween in Hillcrest with an Autumn Fest celebration."

Some vote. Some celebration.

A woman calls out, "So it's all decided then? No more Halloween? No parade? No trick-or-treating?"

"No, actually, ever since we read the committee's report, we've been talking about those very things. And we decided that we ought to keep the costume parade. But every child participating in the parade will be expected to wear a suitable costume. As for trick-or-treating, I think you can see that little kids should not be threatening grown-ups. And we don't exactly favor kids getting all that candy. But that's going to have to be a decision that you parents make. Tell your kids, when they go house to house, to say 'Happy Autumn Fest' instead of 'Trick or treat.' And try to give them healthy snacks instead of candy."

Mr. Steadman calls out, "What about the window painting?"

"I'm glad you brought that up. That's a really important question, and we talked about that, too. Now, we realized that the council can't decide for the merchants what to put on their windows. Anybody who wants their window painted can go ahead and do it. This is still a free country. But we don't think the kids should be taking a day off from school just to slap some paint on store windows. We were all in agreement on this. Painting store windows is just fooling around. So we are going to recommend to the school committee that the children not be given the day off from school for window painting."

Three seats over, I hear Mel gasp, then my mother murmuring to her.

"Now, of course, it'll be up to the school committee to decide, but we think it would be a lot better if the kids took some tests that day—let's see what the kids have been learning."

Some people are nodding their heads and smiling; other people are shaking their heads and frowning. But it doesn't matter what anyone thinks; it's all been decided.

"Now, before we conclude, Mrs. Van Dine has one final comment."

Of course she does.

"Thank you, Mr. Chairman. Some of you have been speaking, rightly, about the things that are bad for children. But tonight, I don't want to dwell on unpleasant matters. I would like you all to leave here tonight with one positive, uplifting thought. Here, in our town of Hillcrest, we are about to offer our children a new holiday, a wholesome way to observe the season, and one that will give us all—adults and children alike—an opportunity to celebrate our American way of life. When, on October thirty-first, our town celebrates Autumn

Fest, we will be saying to the whole world that we are proud to be Americans."

My father's getting ready to leave. I slouch out after him, feeling as if I'm wearing a sandwich board that says: CALLIE JONES, LOSER. Printed on both sides, front and back, so that no one will miss the point.

I'm not the baton twirler in any parade. I'm the clown strutting behind her, thrusting his knees up close to his puffed-out chest, with the soles of his shoes flapping loose in the air, spinning an invisible baton.

Callie's Rules:

- I can make up all the rules I want, but nobody but me will ever follow them.
- And I'll still have to follow other people's rules.

15 A Deep, Deep Mess

Walking home, I hear my mother and father talking in their trust-us-everything's-going-to-be-fine voices. They're wrong. Everything's not going to be fine. This time I've made a bigger mess than I ever made before.

Why didn't I just keep quiet? Let Mrs. Van Dine have her silly Autumn Fest? What difference did it make anyway? Even if we couldn't make a dragon costume, we could have come up with something just as good. Well, maybe not as good as a Chinese dragon—nothing else would ever be that good—but something.

I had to go and shoot off my mouth to half the kids in school, start a petition, get Mr. No-Man mad at me, probably have something in my permanent record. I even got Valeri thinking that Shane is my boyfriend. Shane. I can't face him tomorrow. I just can't. Or anybody else. I got everybody at school—well, maybe not everybody, but 257 of them—all fired up about taking away our Halloween. They'll want to know what happened at the meeting.

What do I tell them? That I never even got to hand in the petition? They'll want to know why, and I'll have to say that the Town Council wouldn't take it because I'm just a kid. And everyone who signed is just a kid. And kids in Hillcrest won't be having Halloween this year.

Hey, it's not my fault. I tried, I really did.

Yeah, try telling that to a bunch of kids after you told them that if enough kids signed the petition we could win. This is the biggest mess I've ever made, and there's nothing I can do but just slosh around in it.

Or maybe not. Maybe I don't have to go back to school tomorrow. I could go visit my grandparents. No, not visit, go live with them. Permanently. That would fix everything. A new school, all new people. I could start over. I could do it right this time.

When we get home, everyone heads to the kitchen for some hot chocolate. Everyone except me. I thud up the stairs to my room and shut the door. I don't know what I'll tell my parents. Maybe I should just write them a note. Later. Right now I need to pack.

My book. I can't leave my book behind. I lift it out of the dresser drawer, where I keep it hidden. My book is really beautiful. As I turn it in my hand, the colors quiver and flow from red to bronze to gold. The spine is bound in brown leather, but inside the pages are creamy, some of them still clean, still not written on. My mother gave me this book, said that I'd know what to write in it. And I did. I love the sounds of words, the look of them on the page. I arrange them, in my head, like beads on a necklace, removing a word, replacing it with another. And when all the words together are perfect and beautiful, I write them down in my book. I bought a pen that writes with bright turquoise ink, and I keep it just to write in my book.

I place the book on top of my dresser and begin to pull out clothes and toss them onto my bed.

Some of the clothes slide off the pile onto the floor. My half of the room, for the first time ever, looks like Mel's.

Until tonight, there might just as well have been a line painted down the middle of the floor. Mel tacks up her drawings all over her walls; my books are lined up neatly in my bookcase. Mel's bed is always a tumble, while mine is always made. And on top of her dresser, Mel keeps the things she's always finding and bringing home, things she loves to look at—dried seedpods and craggy rocks, bits of colored glass and rusted tools, a scrap of kite silk that had caught on a tree branch.

Mel carries things home in her hands and keeps them out where she can see them. I bring things home in my head and hide them away in my book.

Well, I'll be gone in the morning, and Mel can have this whole room to herself. She'll have plenty of places to put her things.

I'm in the closet, starting to pull down my suitcase, when Mel comes into the room and flings herself down on the bed. Now she's mad at me, too. I really have to get out of here. I give the suitcase a yank and it falls to the floor, sending a pile of board games crashing down. Pieces fly everywhere.

Mel looks up, sees me holding the suitcase.

"Callie, where are you going?"

Mel's eyes are wide; her mouth is trembling. She's frightened. When things go wrong, I get mad. Mel gets scared. I sit down next to her on the bed.

"What is it, Mel? What's wrong? It's not the dragon, is it? You'll come up with a sketch for another costume. And you can save your dragon sketch. Maybe you can turn it into a painting or something."

"It's not that, Callie. It's the tests. The day when we were going to paint the windows, they're going to give us tests. Tests! I'm terrible at tests. I get all stiff and my hands shake and I can't even think. I'll do really bad and then everyone will think I'm dumb. I *am* dumb. The only thing I'm good at is drawing and painting. This was going to be my chance to have my design chosen for Halloween window-painting. And now I won't even have that. I hate school!

"Callie, why are you holding your suitcase? Are you running away? Why? Why would you run away? You do great in school."

"You don't understand. Nobody understands. You think school's so great for me? Well, it's not. It's not great at all. I hate it, and I'm never going back."

Mel is quiet for a minute, then she says, "Callie, if you're going away, can I come with you?"

"No! You can't! That's the trouble with this family—too many people. There's always somebody around. I can't even have my own room. I have to share it with a bratty little sister, who puts her stupid pictures up everywhere so I have to look at them."

Mel's face has gone white, and she looks as though someone has kicked her in the stomach and knocked all the air out of her. Which I have. Why do I do these things? It's like my brain is some kind of motor, always racing, and it's out of control. I can't stop it; I can't find the brake. Well, I need to find the brake now. Right now.

"Mel, I didn't mean what I said. You know I didn't. It's just that when you told me that I did great in school, well, you just don't know. I am pretty smart at some things—school things—but pretty dumb at everything else. And what I said just now? That was one of the dumbest things I've ever said.

"Look, I have an idea. You're not dumb. You just don't know the right tricks for taking tests. I do. I could teach them to you. Would you want me to do that?"

"Could you, Callie? No, it wouldn't do any good. I'll still get all stiff and shaky and I'll just look at that test paper and it'll all be just a blur. I can't do it, Callie. I can't."

"Sure you can. You're scared, that's all. I can help you, I promise."

"You promise?"

"Yes. But in return, you've got to help me with my project for art class. Deal?"

"Deal."

Mel and I hook our pinky fingers together. That's the thing about Mel—she gets over things really fast. Not like me. If someone had said those things to me, I'd never forget. I'd just keep rubbing those words across my brain, over and over, until they'd made a permanent groove. I had it backward: Mel's the one who shouldn't have to share a room with me.

Callie's Rules:

• It's better to write things down than to say them out loud. When you write them down, you can change the words later. Or erase them.

"There's one more thing, Mel. Could you help me clean up this mess? I'll do the clothes if you do the games."

Maybe I can clean up the mess in the room, but there's another mess that no one can help me clean up. It's waiting for me at school.

16 No Life to Save

I walk to school the long way, the very long way. If there were an even longer way, I'd take it. On Prospect Street the first ripe chestnuts have fallen to the ground. I could bring some home for Mel. She'd like that. A lot of the chestnuts are still in their spiky husks and or they've been squashed by cars, so I have to peel the husks off the whole ones. Peeling those husks is really painful, and some of the chestnuts inside are lopsided or dented, but finally I find a perfect nut. I slip it into my pocket and rub my fingers over it. This could be a lucky nut. I try a few more, but none of them are as good as that perfect one.

When I reach the school, there's no one outside. I'm really late. I'll have to report to the office and get a pass. The secretary is busy stuffing mailboxes and doesn't see me. But Mr. Nolan does. As he slides past me, he says, "You're late, Calliope."

I know I'm late. That's why I'm here. But before I can ask for a pass, he says, "You'd better get to the auditorium. Your class is already there. Go and sit with them."

The auditorium. Perfect. It's dark in there, and no one will see me come in. Of course, it's so dark I can hardly see. I finally spot my class and an empty seat, on the aisle, next to Alyce. When I sit down, Alyce squirms away from me. I guess she's already heard about last night. Mr. Nolan is up on the stage now, and the teachers are shushing everyone. Maybe that was a lucky chestnut.

"Students, may I have your attention, please. You're about to see a film—an extremely important film, a film that has the potential to save your lives."

He certainly has my attention. Although I'm not sure my life is worth saving.

"Students, I don't need to tell you that we live in very dangerous times. I'm sure that you feel safe in your homes, with your families, in this school, in this town. But you shouldn't. A terrible danger threatens us all: you, your families, this town, our very country. That is the danger of terrorism."

La-dee-dah. I've heard all this before. I know exactly what he's going to say: the terrorists hate our very way of life.

"The terrorists hate our very way of life."

They hate our democracy, our freedoms, our prosperity.

"The terrorists hate our great democracy, our precious freedoms, our enormous prosperity."

Okay, he added a few adjectives. I've still heard it all before. Now Mr. Nolan stops speaking. Is he finished? Can we go now? I hope not. I'd rather stay here in the dark.

"On September eleventh, the terrorists attacked our country, killing thousands of people, leaving wives without husbands, husbands without wives, children without parents, parents without children.

"The terrorists will attack again. They could attack anywhere, at any time. We must all be prepared. The film we're about to show you will help you protect yourselves in the event of an attack. You can protect yourselves and you can be safe. So pay attention and be prepared."

Mr. No-Man slips in the DVD and starts fumbling with the remote. But there's nothing on the screen but flashing black blips. Good. That means we can all stay here a little longer. The lights are turned on, and Mr. Nolan starts saying something about how it'll only take a minute to start the video and will everyone please stay in their seats and we may talk—but quietly.

I wouldn't care if it took all day to start the video, but even Mr. No-Man doesn't need all day to figure out how to work a remote. Looks like I'll have to face this day after all.

As we walk up the aisle, I say to Alyce, "You must be pretty glad that your father built that shelter." I figure I'll get her onto a safe subject before she can say anything about the petition. After all, she already asked me to take her name off it, so why should she care?

Alyce doesn't look at me. "Callie, I don't want you in my shelter. I don't want to be your friend anymore."

I can't answer. I just stare at her.

But Alyce isn't finished. "Callie," she says, and she still doesn't look at me, "you're just too weird."

That word hangs in the air like lightning in the

summer sky, when there's that silent, hold-your-breath pause before the thunder and rain.

"You're weird, Callie. I'm sorry, but you just are." Alyce's face is red, and she looks like she's about to cry. I'm the one who should be crying, not her.

"Go ahead, Alyce. Spit it out. Don't hold back now. What is it? What is it about me that's so weird?"

Now she looks at me, and her voice is all pinched and thin. "It's you, Callie. You're not like everyone else. Look." Alyce pokes at the book I'm holding crooked in my arm. "Look at what you read. *Jane Eyre.* You're always reading books like that. Those are the kinds of books they give you to read in English class in high school. No one reads those for fun. No one but you."

"So maybe if I read *Seventeen* magazine or celebrity rags, I wouldn't be weird? Is that what you're saying?"

"It's not just that, Callie. That petition you had people sign. What was the point of it? It was just stupid, and it made you look stupid—you and everyone else who signed it. I'm just glad I didn't."

The thunder's struck and the rain's coming down in torrents and I can only stand here and drown.

"I don't get you, Callie. Lots of times, when you're in class, I see you moving your lips, like you're talking to yourself, but you don't make a sound. It's like you're a crazy person. You're not normal, Callie."

Alyce thinks I'm weird. What about the others? Do they all think I'm weird? Maybe Alyce is right. I'm not like other people. Maybe I am weird.

It's not my mother. It's not because she's an artist and wears the wrong clothes, cooks the wrong food, finds a barber's chair on the street and brings it home and puts it in the living room. Right next to a dentist's tray. It's not my mother, not my house, not that we have seven kids. Even if I lived in a white sugar cube of a house with a lamp in the front window; even if my mother sold real estate, dyed her gray hair, and wore pretty clothes; even if I were an only child, I'd still be weird.

There's no use thinking of a rule now. It wouldn't help me. Nothing can help me. I'm weird.

17 Two Bloody, Pointing Fingers

I'm really glad that English class is first. Mrs. Thigpen is going to hand back the tests on *Lorna Doone*, and everyone is too concerned about their grades to pay any attention to me. Test grades are one thing I don't have to worry about. Probably the only thing.

Mrs. T places the paper facedown on my desk and I flip it over. *F.* In red ink. Like the scarlet letter, but not an *A*, an *F*. And underneath that *F*, Mrs. T has written, *Please see me after school.*

There's got to be some mistake. This can't be right. I flick my eyes over the test. There's no other comment, just that one accusing *F.* Like two bloody fingers pointing. I stuff the paper into my notebook before anyone else can see it.

F for failure. *F* for fiasco. *F* for fraud. *F* for forsaken by friend. *F* for fool and foolish and fool-hardy.

At least English will be shorter today; all of the classes will, because of the assembly. I just need to make it through to the end of the day, when I can go home and hide. No, I can't. I have to go back into this classroom and face Mrs. Thigpen. *Face* also starts with *F*.

After every class, I have to go out into a hall and walk past several hundred other kids. All day they're after me, asking me about the petition. Sometimes I pretend I don't hear them. But it's no use pretending if the person's standing right next to me. Then I make up some excuse and walk away in a hurry. And then there's gym class, where everyone's watching me miss the basket and the whole teams starts grumbling. Lunch—I won't go near the lunchroom. I head for the library, find a seat in a far corner, and sneak bites of my sandwich from under the table.

After fifth period, Marilyn Shahadi catches up to me in the hall and starts to ask me about the petition. I can't take any more.

"Why are you worried about Halloween?" I snap. "You should be worried about the terrorists!"

Marilyn looks at me like I'm crazy. Maybe I am. Crazy and weird.

Mrs. Thigpen tells me to sit down. I really have to, my legs are shaking so badly.

"Calliope, I assume you know why I asked you to come in this afternoon."

"Yes, Mrs. Thigpen, it's about my test. But I don't understand. I didn't have time to write a conclusion, and I know that might have lowered my grade, but still I don't understand why I got an F. I put in lots of illustrations, just like you asked."

"Just *as* I asked. Yes, you did have a great many illustrations. But all of them were from *Jane Eyre*. In fact, you based your whole answer on *Jane Eyre*. I asked you to write about *Lorna Doone*. You never read it, did you, Calliope?"

"Just the first part." That was strictly true. I did read the first paragraph.

"You obviously didn't read quite enough or you would have realized that the narrator of *Lorna Doone* is not a girl but a boy. And the school he went to was an all-boys' school—a school, not an institution—and the boys did not live at school.

Very few of the illustrations you used would have applied."

"But I thought—"

"You thought, Calliope, that you could choose which book to read, that you could choose which book to write about. But you made the wrong choice. Calliope, you are a very bright young woman. You are thoughtful and articulate. Very often, I would guess, you question authority. That is a good thing to do, not to follow blindly when others tell you what to do. If someone tells you to do something that you know to be wrong, you should not, nor would you, follow them.

"But many times we are told to do something that is neither right nor wrong, but simply a requirement, a rule that must be followed. I must be in school every morning at eight o'clock. Perhaps I've stayed up late the night before, preparing classes, and would prefer to come in to school at ten, but I mustn't do that. So I come to school at the appointed time. Perhaps I would prefer to assign *Jane Eyre* to the class, instead of *Lorna Doone*. But the sixth-grade curriculum requires that I teach *Lorna Doone*, and so I do.

"And when I do, I realize that there are many valuable things in that book as well, things that I will enjoy teaching and discussing with the students.

"What I'm trying to say, Calliope, is that there are good choices and bad. And you need to weigh each choice carefully."

"I understand, Mrs. Thigpen, I really do. I made a mistake. I won't do it again. Could I make up the test? I'll read the book, the whole thing, and I know I'll do better on another test."

"No, that wouldn't be right. If I let you take the test again, after you failed the first one, that wouldn't be fair to the rest of the class, would it? Perhaps then I'd have to let everyone who got less than an A take the test again and try to do better. And what would they have learned? That their choices don't matter? That if they didn't read the assignment, or if they didn't study hard, it didn't matter, because they can always have another go at the test?

"You made your choice, Calliope, and with every choice there are consequences. You'll have to live with the consequences of this choice."

I can't say a word. I can't even look at Mrs. Thig-pen.

"Calliope, I'm afraid I've been sounding a bit harsh. I don't mean to. As I said, you are a very bright girl, and I expect you will do very well in this class. And I am looking forward to that piece of creative writing you're working on. How is that coming by the way?"

Honesty, right now, seems like the best policy.

"To tell the truth, Mrs. Thigpen, I haven't started it yet. I've been kind of preoccupied with another problem."

"I see. Is it something you want to talk about?"

"Thanks, but I think this problem has kind of solved itself. Despite me."

Callie's Rules:

• Truth or Consequences is an old quiz show. But they got it wrong. They should have called it Truth and Consequences. I told the truth and I still had to face the consequences.

Mrs. T says that I need to know when I have

a choice to do something and when I don't. But how can I tell the difference? Sometimes the answer seems so clear to me, I'm so sure I'm doing the right thing, but then it turns out that I was wrong. How can I know what the right choice is?

18 Choices and Consequences

I really want to talk to my mother. I have no idea what I want to talk to her about. Definitely, absolutely, no way am going to tell her I flunked a test.

I will never tell anyone, not as long as I live. Not even if I'm taken hostage by terrorists and they say they'll let me go if I confess my deepest secret to them. Not even then. My shame will be buried with me in my grave.

But right now I want to talk to my mother. Back in the shed, Polly's asleep in her cage. Her head is resting on her favorite blanket. It used to be yellow, with a satin teddy bear in the middle, but it's been washed so many times that the yellow has faded to gray and there's nothing left of the teddy bear but an outline of white stitches. Polly doesn't care. That's still her comfort blanket.

I wish I could just put my head on an old blanket and fall asleep.

My mother hasn't heard me come in. With her gauntleted hands, she's ripping and tearing at something metal.

"Mom, what are you doing? Are you taking apart the new weirdo?"

"Just cutting it down to size."

"But you said this one was going to be tall—that was all you knew about it, that it was tall."

"Well, now I know better. This one's not going to be what I thought it was."

She pulls up her face visor, and her face is as odd and stiff as her voice.

"What is it, Mom? What's wrong?"

She pulls off her gauntlets, reaches behind her protective vest, pulls a folded sheet of paper from her overall pocket, and hands it to me. Then she pulls down her visor, puts on her gauntlets, and goes back to attacking the weirdo.

The paper is yellow and folded in thirds, like a pamphlet. On the front is a bright orange pumpkin. Not a Halloween pumpkin, with scary eyes carved out and grinning teeth, but a perfectly round pumpkin—like no pumpkin ever grown on Earth—with a stem on top. Underneath are the words: WELCOME TO HILLCREST'S FIRST ANNUAL AUTUMN FEST. The letters are dancing, but they lie, like everything else about this stupid holiday.

I already know what's inside this pamphlet, but I have to open it up and read it, like when I know there'll be something really awful coming up in a book, but I turn the page anyway and go on reading. It's as if something is forcing me. What I read inside the pamphlet is really awful. It's all the things Mrs. Van Dine said at the Town Council meeting, except lined up in neat columns and with lots of words in capital letters, just so no one will miss her message.

She has a list of approved costumes—nothing frightening or dangerous, of course, but also nothing any kid who's not a baby or a pampered pet would ever dream of wearing. And "Suggested Treats"—anyone who hands those out and calls them treats had better be prepared for some tricks. At the end she's put a sugary "Closing Message," wishing that everyone will join in the Autumn Fest in a spirit of warmth and fun. Some fun.

My mother raises her visor. "When the mail came and I read that, I was so angry I couldn't work, so I took Polyhymnia to the park and pushed her on the swings. She likes to be pushed really hard and I wanted to push something really hard, so that was fine for a while. But when Polyhymnia wanted to get off the swing and go down the slide, I wasn't calm enough yet to stop pushing, so I made her stay on the swing until she screamed to get off. Some mother, huh? Good thing Sandy Van Dine wasn't around to see that. So I let Polyhymnia off, and then I got on the swing myself and pumped really hard—I could hear the chain clank every time I reached the top of the arc—until I had calmed down a bit.

"When we got back, that little kid was pretty zonked, as you can see, but I suddenly had an idea for a different weirdo this year. And that's the one I'm starting."

"What is it? What will you do?"

"I can't tell you just yet. I'll only say that this one will be a real person, and she'll be life-size."

"But a real person wouldn't be a weirdo. It'll be like something Mrs. Van Dine would approve of. Oh, no, Mom, you're not doing what I think you're doing."

"Just wait, Calliope." Now my mother's smiling. "Wait and see. I think we'll all feel much better when I'm done. I know I will."

I wish that pushing a swing could somehow push out all the mixed-up feelings inside me, or that I could cut them up like pieces of metal. My mother is so strong and sure as she works.

"Mom, don't you sometimes mind being different? Doesn't it bother you?"

She puts down her tools, raises her visor, and looks straight at me. She doesn't say anything for a while. Then she walks over to a couple of lawn chairs against the back wall and motions me to sit beside her.

"Once I did mind, Calliope. I minded a lot. When I was your age, it tormented me. More than anything, I wanted to be like everyone else. I wanted to act the way they did, talk the way they did, like what they liked. And I tried to be just like them. I copied their clothes, their voices; I laughed like them, even carried my books the way they did. I acted as if I was really interested in the things they talked about. But I was always half a step behind them. They always seemed to know what they were doing, to be leading the way, and all I could do was follow them. I made myself crazy, always looking at everyone else to see what I should be doing.

"For a time they let me in, but I was never really a part of them. I don't think they really liked me, they only tolerated me. Because, Calliope, I think they must have known that, no matter how much I tried to be like them, I really was different."

"But, Mom, you always seem so, I don't know, so sure of yourself. You don't seem to care that you're different."

"But I did care, Calliope. I cared very much. I was miserable for a very long time. But eventually, I figured it out. I realized that I could go on being a copy of everybody else, just trailing behind, spending my life as a shadow. Or I could be my own person, walk ahead if I wanted to, take a different path if I wanted to.

"Sweetheart, if everybody acts the same way, feels the same way, thinks the same way, no one will ever have any new ideas, make any new discoveries, create something that's never been created before. Calliope, I finally figured out that you have to be different to make a difference."

My mother reaches for my hand and holds it for a while.

"So what are you saying, Mom? That I have to be miserable? That no one will like me? That I can't have any friends? Or any fun?"

"No, Calliope, I'm not saying that. I'm saying that you have to find friends who will like you for who you are. They are out there, Calliope. You just have to look in the right places."

Right. Look in the right places for friends who will like me for who I am. Where would I find those people? In some dark corner. Or at the rejects table at lunch. My mother doesn't care anymore what other people think. I still do.

Callie's Rules:

- It's no use asking your mother what to do. She'll always give you an answer. But it won't help you.

19 Different Together

My mother doesn't say a word all through dinner. I guess she wants to give us a chance to really enjoy the vegetarian meat loaf. She waits until we've all finished pushing our food around our plates.

"Everyone," she says, "we need to make some decisions. About Halloween. Or what used to be Halloween. Now it seems it's going to be called Autumn Fest. Anyway, we got this today in the mail. From Sandy Van Dine."

She pulls out the yellow paper, unfolds it, and holds it away from her, between two fingers, as though it's something smelly she's taking to the trash.

"I'll just read you some of what it says. There's a list of 'appropriate' costumes. She suggests that children dress as scarecrows, pumpkins, farmers, football players . . . I won't bore you with the whole list. You get the idea. Anyway, she concludes by saying: 'Let's have all our costumes reflect the spirit of autumn in America.'"

"Let's?" My father sounds irritated. "Is Sandy Van Dine planning to wear a costume and join the parade?"

"If she did—" Mel's giggling so hard she can hardly talk. "If she did, she'd have to be a squash. Because she's squashing the whole idea of Halloween."

Everyone laughs. Mel's usually shy, quiet, but now she can't stop talking. "Or she could be a turnip. No one likes turnips."

"Or vegetarian meat loaf." Jack says that, but really quietly so that my mother won't hear.

"Hold on now," my mother says. "Before we get too carried away, I want to read you some of her other suggestions. Here's a list of the costumes that *won't* be allowed in the parade: witches, goblins, ghosts, vampires, skeletons, mummies, clowns—"

"Clowns?" Andy breaks in. "What's wrong with clowns?"

"Some little kids are frightened by clowns. See, she says down here at the bottom that 'no costumes of a frightening, dangerous, or superstitious nature will be allowed in the parade.' I guess that means our dragon won't be allowed in the parade. I'm so sorry, Calliope."

"It's okay. It was a stupid idea anyway."

"It wasn't stupid, Callie. It would have been beautiful."

That's Andy, always trying to be kind. Well, kind won't help me. Not this time. Not when I've gone and stood up at the Town Council meeting, in front of Valeri and everyone, and made a total fool of myself—then been told to sit down and be quiet because I was too young to talk. Not when I went and wrote up a dumb petition and got 257 kids to sign it—257 kids who now know I'm a total jerk—and got Mr. Nolan down on me. Mr. Nolan, who didn't even know my name before, and probably put something bad into my permanent record. *And* I flunked a test! I did all of that in only the first month of middle school. I don't even want to think about what I could do in the rest of the year.

"Calliope?" You can't keep anything from my mother; she notices everything.

"I'm okay, Mom. Go ahead, tell them the rest of it."

"Calliope, you tried. You did your best. But remember that Mrs. Van Dine had Autumn Fest planned out in great detail before she even came to our house. Including what she thinks would be acceptable treats."

Everyone groans. They know what's coming.

"Right. She says that she 'recognizes that people are free to hand out whatever sorts of treats they wish—'"

"It's good to know that this is still a free country, after all." There's Jack again, always going on about free speech, rights, the Constitution.

"Even though people can hand out whatever they wish, she hopes that 'we will all consider the health and well-being of our children and give out only wholesome treats.'"

"As far as I'm concerned," my father says, "Toasty Ghosties are essential to the 'well-being' of our children. In fact, it's been scientifically proven that eating warm, melting chocolate and marshmallows releases endorphins and produces a very strong sense of well-being in the consumer. So kids might really need my Toasty Ghosties again this year. Besides, my pumpkins have grown better than ever this summer. But you kids still have to decide what you want to do about costumes."

"I don't know about the rest of you, and I know I've said this before, that adults are allowed to decide what's best for kids." Jack is off again. "I remember when this first came up, we had that discussion about civil liberties and free speech—"

I'd better shut him up before he starts reading us the Bill of Rights. "Jack, get to the point. Should we wear costumes in the parade or not?"

"No, you shouldn't."

"Well, thanks."

"Don't you want to hear why?"

"Only if you can tell us in fewer than two hundred simple words."

"Okay, then. I don't like Mrs. Van Dine's ideas, and her ideas are the only ones she'll allow, so I don't think we Jones kids should be in her parade. Short and simple enough for you?"

Andy says, "I've been thinking. I could make costumes for all the younger kids, really good costumes that wouldn't be scary or anything, but—"

She stops and looks around the table. "Okay, here goes. I know how hard Callie worked to get that petition signed and all, and I kind of agree with what Jack said, but I think it would be a shame for the kids to miss out on a chance to dress up and march in the parade. Even if it will be boring."

"Melpomene, what do you think?"

Mel answers, so softly that it's hard to hear her, "I was really excited about Callie's dragon idea. I'd made a sketch, with colors and everything. If we're not going to be a dragon, I don't want to be in the parade. Besides, I really was hoping I would get chosen to do window painting."

"That leaves only the twins."

Ted and Fred have been babbling away in their twin talk, but they know they have to speak English to the rest of us.

"We're still going to be a cow," Ted says.

"Yeah, just like we said. We'll paint black spots on a sheet, cut holes for the eyes, make a tail. I'll be the front."

"No, you won't. I'm older. I'll be the front."

"How come you always get to go first? I want to be the head."

"Stop it, boys, this minute. You'll choose up later."

"What about me?" Polly pipes up. "I want to be in the parade."

"Polyhymnia, you're too little to walk in that great big parade by yourself. But you could wear a costume and stand on the sidewalk and wave to everybody as they go by. What would you like to be?"

"I want to be a witch. Like in my book. With a black hat and a green face and a broom."

"She can't be a witch," Andy protests. "That's one of the costumes that's not allowed."

"I am so going to be a witch," Polly insists.

"You can't," I tell her. "Mrs. Van Dine said no scary costumes in the parade."

"Yes, but I can't be in the parade. Mommy says I can stand on the sidewalk in my costume. So if I'm not in the parade, I can be what I want, can't I, Mommy? I want to be a witch. I don't want to wave. I want to scare people."

Sometimes Polly can be a pest, but other times, like now, I just want to hug her.

"It's decided, then," my father says. "Ted and Fred will be in the parade, Polly will wear a costume—a prohibited costume—but she won't march. The rest of you won't participate at all. And I'll still make my Toasty Ghosties."

I look around the table and I see something I've never seen before. Every person in my family is different from everyone else—everyone except the twins, who are very much like each other but not like anyone else.

Oh, sure, we get annoyed with one another. Jack can drive us all crazy with his speeches. Andy's just too perfect. Polly can be awfully bossy. And the twins won't speak English unless we make them. Mel is really shy, and sometimes I get tired of feeling like I always have to protect her.

My father insists on having everything done, as he would say, "precisely and properly." Just the opposite of my mother, who paints our house purple and cooks really odd food.

Callie's Rules:

- Maybe people don't have to be all the same. Maybe we can all be different and still get along. Some of the time.

20 Rules and Regulations

"Cal?"

"Not now, Shane. I have to get to the library before homeroom."

That was a pretty pathetic excuse. Suppose he says he'll walk with me. I should have said I was going to the girls' room. Right. Tell a boy that you're going to the girls' room. Nice thought, Callie. At least he's not coming with me.

But I wish he had. I really would like someone to talk to. It's easy to talk to Shane. He can be a jerk sometimes. Like when he does that can-I-go-pee? thing. But even so, he's smart. And he hates Valeri and this whole Autumn Fest thing as much as I do. It might be nice to have Shane for a friend.

But I can't.

My mother would say, "Of course you can,

Calliope. You like Shane. Why can't you two be friends?"

See? That's why I can't talk to my mother. She was never in middle school. Well, I guess she was, but that was a long time ago. Everything was different then. She doesn't know how things are now. I usually don't know how things are, either, but one thing I do know. If people see me talking with Shane, they'll start to say he's my boyfriend. And that's not allowed. Not for me. In sixth grade, only the popular girls can have boyfriends. If anyone else does, they make fun of them.

No, I absolutely cannot stand around and talk to Shane before school. It might be okay, though, if we talked when we're walking between classes. Then it would look like we were just heading to the same class and started to talk. But I definitely can't sit with him at lunch. Boys sit at boys' tables and girls sit at girls'. And not even popular girls can break that rule.

Rules. Everything in middle school is rules. The principal makes rules, the teachers make rules, and the kids make their own rules. It's not just school. Parents make rules. The Town Council makes rules.

Of course, I do, too. But mine are different. I don't make anyone else follow my rules. Come to think of it, I don't follow them, either.

Callie's Rules:

- Sometimes you have to break your own rules. But only if you want to.

Today, my rule for myself is to keep away from Shane. And I'm determined not to break this one. I duck out quickly after English. He calls after me, but I act like I don't hear him and just keep walking—fast. It's like that all day, but after science, he catches up with me.

"Cal, did you see this morning's paper?"

"No, my father always takes it with him to read on the train. Why, what's in it? Something about Autumn Fest?"

"No, worse. A *lot* worse. It's the weirdos."

"The weirdos! Shane, what are you talking about? They wouldn't be in the paper; we haven't even put them up yet."

"It doesn't look like you will be putting them up this year. I can't talk now, I'll be late for

Spanish. Look in the paper when you get home."

I race home, but, just as I said, my father's taken the paper with him. All I can do is wait until he gets home. When he does, I know that he's already read it—whatever it is.

"Callie, call everyone into the living room, please. And get your mother, too."

I want to tell him that I know it's about the weirdos, ask him what's going on, but his face looks like a storm's coming, and so I run to the back door to ring the cowbell, calling all the kids as I go.

The kids are taking their time showing up, probably because it was me calling, so I try again. This time I tell them to hurry up, that Dad's looking mad. In a couple of seconds, everyone's there. Everyone except my mother and Polly. I know my mother has to put her work away, but I wish she'd hurry up.

Finally, we're all in the living room. No one says a word. They can see something's wrong.

"I want to read you something in today's paper," my father says. Then he stops, looks at the younger kids, and says, "No, let me tell you. The Town Council has voted to ban all fixed structures in front yards. Ban means they won't allow them. Oh, they make exceptions for mailboxes, outdoor lights, birdbaths, things like that, but everything else is prohibited."

The other kids are looking at him with quizzical faces. They don't understand. But I do.

"It's the weirdos, isn't it, Dad?" I ask. "They don't want us to put up the weirdos on Halloween."

"Possibly, Callie."

The kids don't look confused now. Everyone is talking at once.

"Kids," my father cuts in, "we'll never be able to discuss this if we don't talk one at a time."

"They can't do that, can they?" Fred asks.

Then Ted finishes for him, "The weirdos belong to us."

"Yes, boys. The weirdos do belong to us, but the town can decide what structures can be put up in front yards. It's called zoning regulations."

"Maybe Callie's wrong," Andy puts in. "The Town Council didn't specifically say no weirdos. Maybe they meant, oh, I don't know, maybe they meant things like old cars and junk like that. Awful-looking stuff."

"Andy, they've already got regulations against junk and old cars." Jack, as usual, knows everything. "This is something new."

Mel is saying softly, "First they won't let us paint the store windows and now they won't let us put up the weirdos. They're spoiling everything."

"Dad," I say, "why can't we put up the weirdos? We'll put them up on Halloween afternoon and take them down again the next morning. We'll all get up really early to do it. What can they do then? Tell us to take them down? They'll already be down."

"They can fine us, Callie. They will fine us fifty dollars for each structure for each day it stands. Eighteen weirdos—if Mom finishes the one she's working on—at fifty dollars apiece, that's nine hundred dollars a day. Sounds pretty expensive for one night's fun."

See? Everything in the world goes according to rules. The rules rule.

21 Breaking Rules

I'm mad. Really mad. I was mad all night, and I'm still mad this morning. I guess it shows. Mrs. Thigpen stops me on my way out of class to ask if everything is all right. I say I'm fine. Alyce has been looking at me funny, and Shane doesn't even try to talk to me. That's okay. I'm too mad to talk to anyone today.

Until third-period social studies. I've only half been paying attention—something about settlers and Indians. And then I hear the word *movement*. *Movement!* There's a sudden picture in my brain. I see it, and it's perfect and beautiful. I have to tell someone right now.

Except I can't burst out in the middle of class and say, "Excuse me, Mr. Steinmetz, but I have an announcement to make." Anyway, the other kids wouldn't have any idea what I'm talking about.

But I do have to tell *someone*. And I don't care how many rules I break. At lunch, I march right over to the boys' side of the cafeteria, to the table where Shane is sitting. Table by table, all the other kids stop eating and stare. I've just broken an unbreakable rule: Girls stay on one side of the cafeteria, boys on the other. Shane turns around, and his face looks as if a worm has just crawled out of the apple he's eating.

"What's worse," I ask him, "than finding a worm in your apple?"

The cafeteria is dead quiet. Even Shane can't speak.

"Finding half a worm in half an apple."

Shane looks down in horror at his apple.

"Sorry about that. One of the twins' jokes. But Shane, I need to talk to you." There goes another rule: Girls should always play hard to get.

"Can you come to dinner tonight?" Now it's like I've broken all Ten Commandments. At once. But I don't care. From now on, I follow my own rules.

Shane's mouth is open, but he doesn't say a word.

"I can't guarantee that we'll have anything you'll want to eat, but you have to be there when I tell my family."

I can just imagine what they're all thinking—what they'll all be saying—about what I'm going to announce tonight. This is getting to be fun.

Shane manages to stammer an "O-kay." Then he turns dark red and mumbles, "But I have to check with my mother first."

It's kind of nice to be embarrassing other people for a change.

"Six o'clock," I tell him. Then I turn and march out of the room.

What did they put in my lunch? I didn't see any tag on my sandwich that said EAT ME. Or on my milk that said DRINK ME. But I've definitely turned into someone I wasn't before. I've just broken about a law book's worth of rules (rules even I knew!), and I don't care.

I don't care that for the rest of the day, people are staring at me, whispering about me. I don't care that Alyce won't even look at me. I don't care. I do care that the other boys are poking Shane with their elbows and saying things to him. I really like Shane and maybe I shouldn't have embarrassed him that way. But every time I think about what I did, what I said, I want to laugh. In the middle of science class, remembering what happened, I actually do laugh. Out loud.

Whoops! *Okay, Callie, get a grip. You may be carrying this breaking-the-rules thing too far.*

22 The Side Row

That night, everyone in my family tries to act like it's no big deal that Shane's coming to dinner. But of course it is. No one brings a boy home to dinner, at least no sixth-graders.

I never knew it could be so much fun, breaking rules. I'm starting to think that if you can't be one of the people who makes the rules, you ought to be one of the people who breaks them. Well, the stupid rules anyway. The ones that exist only to make the rule makers feel good. Like telling people what costumes they can wear on Halloween. Or not allowing "fixed structures in front yards." Those rules ought to be broken. And the rule that a boy can't have dinner at a girl's house is a very stupid rule and there is no reason why I shouldn't break it.

When I open the door, Shane looks terrified.

He's clutching a box of candy with both hands.

"My mother said I should take this."

"Right. I can see that you took it." This is getting good.

"I mean, she wanted me to give this to your mother."

"Okay, then. Come on in and give it to her."

Shane looks as if he'd rather turn and run, but he does come in. And he manages to whisper, "This is for you . . . Mrs. Jones." But he's still gripping the box, and my mother practically has to pry it from his hands.

I'm actually starting to feel sorry for Shane, but Jack comes to the rescue.

"Shane," he says, "would you like to shoot some hoops until dinner's ready?"

When we ring the cowbell for them, Shane is starting to look more like himself.

But I'm not at all like myself. I can't hold back another instant. As soon as everyone is sitting at the table, I burst out, "We're going to make our dragon! And I know how."

"No, we're not," Andy objects. "We did know how we were going to make it. We had a design and everything. But they won't allow a dragon in the parade, so that's the end of it."

"It would have been beautiful," Mel says, "but it won't ever be. It's all over."

"No, it's not," I say. "Just listen to my idea."

"*You* listen, Callie," Jack interrupts. "The dragon costume is out. There's no point in our putting all that work into a costume and then having them throw us out of the parade."

"Calliope," my mother says, in her I-know-you're-upset-but-when-you're-older-you'll-understand voice. "Calliope, there can't be any dragon costume this year, and there won't be any weirdos, either."

"The jury's still out on my Toasty Ghosties," my father says. Always the lawyer talk.

"There will so, too, be a weirdo this year—a dragon weirdo."

"Callie," Jack looks really mad. "The weirdos are out. Not a dragon and not any of the other seventeen weirdos. We heard your idea for putting up the weirdos on Halloween afternoon and taking them down the next morning. But unless you've got nine hundred dollars to throw away . . ."

"Will you people just be quiet for a minute and listen? The rule says no fixed structures. Right. That's the point. Our dragon won't be 'fixed.' It'll move."

Everyone is looking at me, but I can see they don't yet understand. Except for one person—Shane. He looks a cartoon character with a light-bulb over his head. Except that Shane looks as though the bulb just lit up inside him.

"Callie," he says, "that's brilliant. It'll be a lot of work, but if we all do it together—"

"Callie," Jack interrupts, "I still don't get it. I understand that we can all wear a dragon costume and that we'll be moving. But what does that have to do with the weirdos? And we can't wear the cos-tume in the parade anyway."

"Okay, here goes. Now listen carefully. We're not going to make a dragon costume. We're going to make a dragon weirdo. And it will move across the yard. Do you get it now?"

"I think I do," my mother says slowly, a tiny smile starting at her eyes. "But how do we make it move across the yard? I think that's beyond even my most creative abilities."

"That's not hard." Shane is all excited now, not at all shy anymore. "There can be a bicycle, underneath the head. I'll pedal. And pull the rest of the dragon behind."

"It'll have to be very lightweight," my father puts in. He's all excited now, too. "So that you can pull it."

"I'll make an aluminum armature and the sides out of plastic mesh," my mother says. "That'll be very light. And we'll need wheels under the feet and tail."

"Wait!" Andy shouts out. "Pet-food cans. At the animal shelter. If I take off the lids and the bottoms and clean them really well, we can attach them to the mesh, overlapping, like scales Oh, no. I can't. They recycle all their cans."

"Of course you can take them," Jack says. "We're supposed to reuse, repurpose, recycle. All three are perfectly acceptable options. We'll be doing two out of the three, Andy."

Jack's right, but I'd never tell him so.

"And we can paint the scales—beautiful, shimmering colors." Mel looks happy again.

"Don't throw away the sides of the cans," Jack

adds. "I can link them together for the dragon's tail."

"Hold on a minute," my father says. "Let me go get a pad and paper. We need to write this all down, assign everyone jobs, establish a schedule."

When my father says the word *schedule*, it's as though a blast of frigid air just blew through the room.

"We can't do it," Andy moans. "Today's September twenty-fourth. We won't have enough time."

"Yes, we will," my mother says. "If we all work together—all of us, including Shane—we can be done in time."

I look at Shane. He's grinning. He'll do it.

"I'll make the head and the framework for the body while you all are in school. But after school and on weekends, the eight of you, and Dad, can work on the scales, and the tail, and whatever else we need."

"Wait. One more thing."

Everyone is looking at me and for a minute I'm too scared to say what I want to say. But if I'm a girl who could ask a boy to dinner, in front of the whole cafeteria, I can do this.

"I'd like to write a play. For the dragon. And we can all be in it."

"Me, too?" Polly asks.

"Of course you'll be in it."

"I can dance. I'll wear my pink tutu and I'll dance."

"Polly, I think the only one dancing will be the dragon, but I can guarantee you that you'll have a part. A really good part."

"Our little acting company will need a name," my father says. "Any suggestions?"

"We can't call it the Weirdo Theater," Andy says. "No one will come."

"We'd have to be draggin' 'em in," Jack says.

I grab my father's pad, take a fresh page, and write at the top, *WEIRDOS*. Then I scramble the letters around in my head.

"I've got it. I know what to call it. We'll call ourselves the Side Row Theater."

Everyone looks puzzled.

"Side Row. It's an anagram for *Weirdos*." I'd better explain to the little kids. "An anagram is when you take all the letters in a word and switch them around to make a new word. I took the letters in *weirdos*, switched them around, and came up with *Side Row*. It's just right. Everyone wants to sit in the center rows; they think it's the best place to be. But when you sit on the side, you get to see all the other people and you get a different view. I think it's better on the side."

"A vote," my father says. "All in favor of calling our production the Side Row Theater, raise your hands. Good, that's it then. We are now officially the Side Row Theater Company."

23 Madness

In the middle of the night, it hits me, hits me so hard I wake up sweating. They say that when you die, your see your whole life again. What I'm seeing is just one scene, me marching over to the boys' side of the cafeteria, right up to Shane, cracking my stupid joke about a worm in an apple, ordering him, actually ordering him, to come to dinner. I don't have to see my whole life. That one scene was bad enough.

What happened? I started out mad, but then I went mad—as mad as that lunatic woman in the tower. I wanted to be like Jane, and I turned into her opposite, the mad woman. True, I didn't set a fire, or burn a house down, the way the mad woman did, but I might as well have set fire to my life.

If I had set a fire, if I had burned the school

down, I wouldn't have to go back there tomorrow. Everyone will be talking about me, saying what a crazy person I am. But what did I do? What did I really do that was so terrible? There's no wall down the middle of the cafeteria, no sign that says: BOYS ONLY. NO GIRLS MAY ENTER HERE.

So I broke a rule, so what? I didn't burn the school down. I only broke one of those ridiculous rules they have. Some rules make sense. Like the school rules about fire drills. Or grown-ups telling little kids not to play with matches. But rules can't protect us from everything. Mr. Kane's survival shelter won't stop an attack. And Mrs. Van Dine's Autumn Fest won't keep kids from having nightmares.

That was Mrs. Van Dine's idea for Autumn Fest—forbid anything scary and then all the kids will be safe. I mean, maybe she meant well. She wants to protect us. But that's not the way to keep us safe. There are real things out there that can really hurt us—and wearing happy costumes won't make those things go away.

Well, I know what I need to say, and I'm going to say it, say it all in my play.

I take my beautiful book and my turquoise pen out of my dresser and start down the stairs, walking on the edge of the steps so they don't creak. I sit down at the kitchen table and begin to write—not in my book, just on a pad. When I have the play just the way I want it, then I'll copy it into my beautiful book.

24 A Strange, New Land

My mother and Mel draw the design for the dragon, and everyone helps to build it. Even Shane. But not little Polly. My mother gives her a paint-brush and some paints, and she sits inside her cage painting pictures of dragons. She says we can put them up on all the front windows of the house.

Before anything else, my mother needs to mea-sure Shane on his bicycle so that the dragon's body will cover him. Andy goes off to the animal shelter to collect their empty pet-food cans. When there aren't enough, Jack drives her to the shelters in other towns to collect their cans. Mel decides that the scales should be of different sizes, with the larg-est ones at the top, tapering down to the smallest, so Andy and Jack go to restaurants and diners for their cans. Then the two of them scrub the cans clean—my mother gives them work gloves to wear so that they don't cut their hands—and set them out in the backyard to dry. We all paint.

When all the scales have been painted, we punch holes in them and link them together with little copper S hooks. They cascade like a shimmering waterfall.

Every day the dragon grows more beautiful. Curling horns sprout from its narrow head, and its red eyes gleam. There are claws at the end of each of its four legs, and its tail is a spiral. But the most wonderful thing is the dragon's body. From its long neck to its tail, its body is covered in scales that gleam like precious jewels—rubies and emeralds, sapphires and pearls—and like gold and silver and amber. We turned those dirty, smelly old cans into something beautiful.

We're all working together, but I'm in charge, writing the play, directing the rehearsals. And as I write, something happens to me. I'm changing, just like those cans. It's as though the dragon has become part of me. I feel myself growing stronger, bolder. Like the dragon. The dragon is urging me on to a strange new place. When

I'm writing my play, I'm living in that place.

We print up announcements and post them all over town.

The Side Row Theater Company
Presents
A Special Performance by a Dazzling Dragon
On Sunday, November 1, at 7:00 P.M.
3 Potter Place
Refreshments will follow.

(My father added that last part, said the offer of food would be sure to bring in the crowds.)

As we tack up the posters, two terrible ideas are clashing in my head. One part of me thinks, *Suppose no one comes.* I can see us all, in our costumes, the dragon in his shining splendor, and no one, not one person, comes to see the play. What then?

But supposing they all come, all of them, the entire town comes and stands there on the sidewalk in front of 3 Potter Place. And then I'll have to step forward, in front of them all, and let them see my play. Both possibilities are terrifying.

25 Autumn Fest

It's finally Halloween—oops, sorry—Autumn Fest. The grown-ups are gathering on Hillcrest Avenue, waiting for the parade to begin. The street just doesn't look as happy as it used to on Halloween—no bright pictures painted on the store windows, only the usual displays of shoes, shampoo, and plumbing.

The kids are all tumbling around in the middle of the street—it's been blocked to traffic—and Mrs. Van Dine is flitting about, trying to get the kids into some kind of order. No one's paying much attention. Just when she gets a kid into what she thinks is the right place, the kid sees a friend and walks away, or another kid will lose part of his costume and run crying to his parents to fix it.

Suddenly, Mrs. Van Dine spots our family on the corner where we're standing. Her face freezes, and she starts toward us.

"Mrs. Jones," she says, and she's practically screaming, or as close to screaming as her perfect self ever comes, "I thought you understood. We can't have any frightening costumes in the Autumn Fest parade."

She's looking at Polly, who's wearing her witch suit, with her face painted a bright, ghoulish green, waving her little play broom around and shouting, "Boo!"

"Oh, I understand completely, Sandy," my mother says, and it's funny, but now she sounds just like a perfect person. "I do understand your rules. But Polyhymnia isn't in the parade. She's only standing here on the sidewalk. And as far as I know, as long as she's fully dressed, she's not breaking any laws—no matter what she's wearing."

"Yes, but"—Mrs. Van Dine is so angry she's sputtering—"her witch costume. It might frighten the other children."

My mother starts to laugh.

"Mary, I don't know why you should think this

is funny. I'm quite serious. We can't allow the children to become frightened."

"Sandy, I'm laughing because, when I think that a little four-year-old girl, with her face painted green, yelling 'Boo' might frighten anyone . . . I'm sorry, the whole thing just seems quite funny to me."

For the first time that I can remember, Mrs. Van Dine is speechless.

I look at her perfect chocolate-ice-cream hair, her perfect camel-colored jacket, her perfect leather pants and boots, and then I look back at my mother, in her not-so-perfect plaid jacket and jeans and sneakers, and a funny idea strikes me. Mrs. Van Dine isn't really trying to be mean, she needs things to be perfect because she gets upset when they aren't—not just upset, maybe even a little scared. When everything is perfect, she's sure that nothing bad can creep in. But my mother gets upset when things *are* perfect. My mother likes to keep things free and open, to leave room for the possibility of something different.

And me? I guess I'm somewhere in the middle. I'll never be perfect like Mrs. Van Dine, but

I don't think I'll ever be as free as my mother. I'm too much of a worrier.

Mrs. Van Dine whirls around and goes back to arranging the marchers in what she thinks is the appropriate order. The twins are dressed in their cow costume. They've taken an old sheet, painted black spots on it, cut out holes for the eyes, painted on a mouth, and attached a rope tail. They blackened their boots with shoe polish, but a lot of the yellow still shows through. Mrs. Van Dine puts the cow-twins behind a scarecrow and places a farmer next to them.

I hear her say, "There, that makes a very attractive autumn grouping."

It doesn't look like she's ever going to get all the kids to stay where she puts them, so finally she just walks up to the front of the parade, where Valeri is waiting to lead. Suddenly, there's a bit of a commotion coming from halfway down. The scarecrow who was supposed to be in front of the cow-twins has burst out crying, and he's running to his mother.

Mrs. Van Dine hurries back to see what the trouble is.

"It was him," the boy screams. "The cow. The cow was eating my straw."

"Both of you, you're out of the parade."

Ted yanks back his half, the front half, of the costume and says, "I didn't eat his straw, I only licked it. Besides, we're a cow. Cows eat straw."

We can hardly keep our faces straight. Even Polly is laughing.

Mrs. Van Dine won't allow the twins back in the parade, and the scarecrow won't stop crying, so the farmer has to walk by himself. Looks like the twins have spoiled Mrs. Van Dine's "attractive autumn grouping." What a shame.

She hurries back to Valeri, who takes off her coat and hands it to her mother. Valeri has decked herself out in a high-school cheerleader's outfit, a thick white sweater, with a large letter *H* sewn on the front, and a flippy blue skirt—the Hillcrest High School colors—and she has on white socks and bright, white sneakers, and now her mother hands her a megaphone.

Valeri puts the megaphone to her mouth and calls out, "Give me an *H*!"

Behind her, the kids, in clumps and clusters,

are fidgeting or waving to their parents. No one answers her call.

Valeri tries again. "Give me an *H*!"

From the sidewalk, a few parents call back, *"H."*

Valeri's gotten all the way to the first *L* and still none of the kids is paying any attention to her. On the sidewalks, mothers are calling out, "Over here, look over here," while the fathers are snapping pictures.

Now Mrs. Van Dine whips the megaphone away from her daughter.

"May I have your attention, please," she commands. "The parade is about to start. Let's all give a proper cheer for the town of Hillcrest."

She hands the megaphone back to Valeri. This time the kids answer when she calls out her letters, but they don't answer in unison. The cheer sounds more like, "Aitch-aitch-aitch . . . aitch." "Aye, aye . . . aye." Still, she does make it through all the letters, and then the parade starts down the street.

It's a pretty dull parade. But the time the fifty-second football player has passed by, most of the parents have put away their cameras and aren't even watching. The refreshments at the high school aren't much better. There are still cups of cider, but no doughnuts. Just bags of pretzels.

I take Polly, in her banned witch costume, and the twins, in their banned-from-the-parade cow costume, trick-or-treating. Except they're not allowed to call it that. At each house, they have to say, "Happy Autumn Fest."

It's kind of sad at our house afterward. My father didn't even make his Toasty Ghosties. He said Toasty Ghosties without the weirdos just didn't seem right. Everyone watches as Polly and the twins empty their bags onto the table.

"I only got three little pieces of candy," Polly wails. "And they're not what I like."

The twins look at each other and say, "Ugh-o." Everyone understands what that means.

There isn't much candy. A lot of apples. A few boxes of raisins. One bag of cold popcorn. Several toothbrushes. Pencils. And one family had given out little slips of paper with fortunes on them. But just a few sad pieces of candy that the kids have to dig out of their piles on the table, like homeless people searching in Dumpsters.

I remember when we'd all empty our bags onto the table and start the serious business of trading.

"I'll give you my nougat bar for two of your almond bars."

"Uh-uh! I'm not giving you two for one."

"Okay, who wants to trade for my chocolate-covered raisins?"

Mel hates raisins, won't eat them even covered with chocolate.

The trading would go on for at least an hour. Afterward, we'd each pick out two or three candies for that night, then hook the handles of our bags over the backs of our chairs, to keep for the next nights, saving the best candies for last.

Callie's Rules. The Things Kids Can Learn from Halloween Candy:

- When kids trade, they learn that candies have different values. They're learning economics.

- When kids save their candy, to make it last longer, they're getting character training.
- Kids don't fight when they're trading. They're learning cooperation.

26 A World of Wonders

While I'm spreading the white makeup over my face, I don't let myself think about what's outside, about *who's* outside. I keep talking to myself, giving myself instructions: *You need a little more at the sides. Be careful under the eyes. Don't forget your neck.* When I stop talking and start thinking, I get scared. My whole body shakes. Are you done? Look carefully. Did you miss any spots? No. Okay. Pull up your hood.

And when I do that, when I pull the deep hood of my long, gray cloak up over my head, suddenly I'm not afraid anymore. Just as it always used to be on Halloween, when I put on a costume, I'm not Calliope Jones, I'm not different, I'm not weird. I'm someone else, and I'm not scared.

I take one last look around the shed—everyone is ready—and I step out and walk slowly to the front yard. A wide circle of lighted candles marks the stage. I walk across to the middle and take my place beside the clump of white birches.

I have to know—did anyone come? I look out over the candles, and I can hardly believe it. People are everywhere: on the sidewalk, spilling into the street, on every side of the yard. They've come. I can't see their faces, but I can see that most of them are kids, and there are grown-ups, too. Why did the grown-ups come? Were they expecting a real theater company? Will they be disappointed? Have I made another terrible mistake? Well, if I have, I'll just have to live with it.

I look up at the attic window, where my father is standing. I nod my head, and from the window comes the distant sigh of wind chimes. The crowd falls silent.

I unroll the scroll I'm holding, and I begin to read:

Listen closely to my words. I am about

to recount for you the strange tale of the dragon.

My tale takes place long ago, so many years ago that no one now alive can remember when.

In a valley, beneath tall mountains, lay a small village. Each day the villagers went about their work.

This is their cue and they all—my sisters and brothers, my mother, all of them in the same gray cloaks, appear, miming the work of the villagers: digging, chopping, stirring, weaving.

But one day, something—something unspeakable—frightened the people of the village. They took flight and found refuge in a cave at the base of a mountain.

They run, looking fearfully over their shoulders, then they cluster together at the far end of the yard.

Years passed, and the villagers remained

in the cave, working, eating, sleeping there.

Once again the actors take up the digging, chopping, stirring, weaving that they had done before.

Children were born in the cave and old people died there. In time, the villagers' sight grew dim. They could see only shadows, shades of gray. For light, they knew only the pale glow of the moon that, each month, when it was full, shone into the mouth of their cave. Then they shielded their eyes, which burned and ran with tears. And gradually, the people could no longer remember light, lost all memory of color.

Then one night, as the moon was rising—

From the attic window, a round white light appears, shining down on the villagers below.

—a fearsome creature appeared at the entrance to the cave.

As I say these words, the dragon begins to glide slowly into the yard.

The dragon sparkled with light and gleamed with color, and the villagers were very much afraid. They threw stones at the dragon, hurled tools at it, and the dragon turned and fled.

The dragon slowly turns and disappears around the corner of the house. The moonlight darkens.
I wait for a moment. No one makes a sound. Then the moon again brightens.

At the next full moon, the dragon returned. And, as before, the villagers were terrified. But one very small girl, who had been born in the cave and had never seen such a wondrous sight, began to move toward the creature.

Now Polly, the smallest of the villagers, leaves the others and walks timidly toward the dragon.

The villagers are struck with terror; they reach out to her, implore her to return. But they will not follow her, will not leave the cave.

"Come back," they call. "Come back."

But it is as though the dragon has cast a spell over the child. She does not hear them.

"Cover your eyes!" they call. "Cover your eyes. That is a fearsome creature. You must not look at it."

And once again they hurl tools and sticks at the dragon and drive it away.

For the second time, the dragon slips away, and the moonlight is extinguished.

I wait for a few moments. There is no sound but the call of a distant owl. Then the moon once again shines down.

On the third full moon, the dragon once

more appeared. And once more the little girl was drawn toward him.

"Get back," the villagers cried. "Come away. We must kill the dragon so that it never returns."

But the little girl did not hear them. She stepped close to the dragon and held out her hand to it. The villagers shrieked and cried and moaned. They raised their tools and beat on the walls of the cave to frighten the dragon away.

From high in the attic comes a loud pounding sound.

But, as the dragon slowly turned away from the cave, the little girl started after it.

Then the people called out to her, "No, no. You must not leave the cave. There are terrible things in the world outside, things unknown to us, hideous things."

"To be sure," the girl called back, "the dragon is strange, but it is not hideous. I think it is beautiful. There must be other beautiful things in the world outside. I want to see them."

As the dragon slithers out of the yard and around the corner of the house, the little girl flings off her cloak. Underneath, she is wearing a dress of brilliant colors. Leaving her cloak on the ground, the child follows the dragon.

Once again the moon darkens, leaving the scene lighted only by the wavering candles.

The villagers called to the girl, implored her to return, but they would not venture beyond the cave. They returned to their darkness. And the little girl was never seen again.

Now I throw back my own hood and look straight out at the assembled audience and say,

If you want to see the little girl and her dragon, follow them, follow them beyond the cave and discover a world of wonders.

All this time, the audience has been silent, has scarcely moved, but now they are like a held breath that is suddenly let out, and they rush after the dragon. Then from the backyard comes a wild whooping, whistling, yelling.

I feel as though I'm too tired to ever move again and also as though I want to run and run forever. I follow the crowd to the backyard. On every side are the weirdos—all seventeen of them, tall, small, glowing, glowering, blowing smoke. And in the middle of them all, still and proud, stands the wonderful dragon.

Suddenly, someone calls out, "There she is," and everyone turns to me and begins to cheer and clap.

For me. They're cheering and clapping for me—Calliope Jones. I grab hold of everyone—my sisters and brothers; my mother; Shane, who's crawling out from under the dragon, my father, who's just coming out the back door of the house. My father says, "It's time for a bow." And we all hold hands together and bow. Everybody cheers and claps again.

Then a loud, whining voice breaks through. "What are you all doing here? Can't you see? Those creatures are horrible; they're ugly and frightening. You shouldn't be here. None of you should be here."

"Shut up, Valeri." That's Shane! "You're the one who shouldn't be here. Why did you come anyway?"

"If you've worked up an appetite," my father breaks in—he knows what's needed right now— "if you're all hungry, I've got a fresh batch of Toasty Ghosties for you all. Nothing better on the night after Halloween than a mass of ectoplasm, on top of a flattened bat, between two coffin lids."

Shane pokes me in the arm and points to the side of the house. Valeri is storming off, and stuffing a Toasty Ghostie into her mouth. My own mouth is so filled up with gooey, warm sweetness that I can't even laugh.

27 Applause, an Apology, and an Attack

As I walk to school, a misty gray rain is trickling from the bare tree branches, and the sidewalks and streets are slick with sodden leaves. But to me the raindrops might as well be rays of sunshine and the fallen leaves cherry blossoms.

The walkway and steps outside the school are deserted. Everyone's clustered inside the doors.

"Cool show, Callie!"

"The dragon was amazing. The most amazing thing I've ever seen."

"The weirdos were really spooky. The whole thing was. I really liked it."

"Callie, I didn't go to the show last night, but I heard it was great. Will you be doing it again?"

I don't know who to answer first. I just whip around from one kid to the next, grinning like a jack-o'-lantern. Then I feel someone take hold of my arm. Alyce is standing next to me.

"Callie . . . Callie . . . I saw the show last night. And—"

"And what, Alyce? You thought it was weird? Like me?"

"No, that's not what I was going to say."

"Oh, what were you going to say? Go ahead, tell me. I already know you think I'm weird. What else is on your mind?"

"You don't have to be so mean, Callie."

"Mean? Me? You're the one who was mean, Alyce. You used to be my friend."

"Okay, if you want to be like that, fine."

Alyce starts to walk away, but before she turns, for just a moment, there's a look on her face like the one on Mel's, the night I yelled at her.

"Alyce?"

She looks back at me.

"I don't want to be like that," I say. "I'm, I'm sorry." Boy, was that ever hard for me to say.

"Callie? I'm sorry I said you were mean."

"That's okay, Alyce. You wanted to tell me something?"

"Yeah, I did. I was going to tell you that I thought the dragon was really beautiful. And I thought Valeri was really nasty last night, the things she said. And, well, I know you'll think I'm dumb, Callie, but I didn't really understand the play, all about the villagers and the little girl. And I was hoping . . . Never mind. It's not important."

"No, go ahead, Alyce. You were hoping what?"

"I was hoping maybe you could explain it to me."

My mother said I should find friends who like me for who I am. Maybe Alyce still does.

"Yeah, I guess I could. Later. Do you want to go to Cubby's this afternoon? If we run, maybe we can get there in time to get a seat. You save us a place and I'll order the Cokes—one cherry and one lemon-lime."

Alyce grins.

Callie's Rules:

- If everybody liked their Coke the same way, the world would be a pretty boring place.

Mrs. Thigpen is at her desk, correcting some papers. I'd planned to wait until Friday, when everyone will be working on the sentence-structure unit and I was supposed to be working on my special assignment, but suddenly I can't hold back even a minute.

"Mrs. Thigpen? I've finished."

Mrs. Thigpen looks up, and I fish around in my loose-leaf notebook, find the play, and hand it to her.

"It's a play. Of course, this is only the words. There were costumes. And music and lights. I've written all that into the script, so you can see where they go. But oh, the dragon. You should have seen it, Mrs. Thigpen. The dragon was my idea, but everyone worked on it. Shane, too. It was so beautiful. I wish you could have seen it."

"I did see it, Calliope."

"You did?"

"Yes, I was there last night. I wasn't going to miss an opportunity to see a new theater company in our town. The Side Row Theater Company, I think it was?"

"Yes, that's an anagram, for *weirdos*. Those are the sculptures my mother makes. Did you see them, too? That's how this whole thing started."

And before I can stop myself, I'm telling Mrs. Thigpen the whole story. Then the bell rings and I'm starting to my desk, when Valeri walks in and plants herself right next to me, blocking my way.

"That little play you put on last night," she hisses, "was really awful. You were in it, so you couldn't see how really awful it was. You thought everyone liked it, but they were really only mocking you. They thought you were a joke."

"You really are pathetic, Valeri, a pathetic and very small person."

"Do you know how ugly you looked, Callie Jones? With your pasty white face? And that tacky, gray thing you were wearing?"

"I wrote what I wanted to say, Valeri, and there's nothing you can do about it now."

"Oooh, just you wait, Callie. You think it's all over, but it's not. Just wait."

28 Charms

Valeri is right. It isn't over. A week later, a letter arrives from the Hillcrest town hall, addressed to Herman Jones. My father calls us all together and reads the letter to us. It informs Mr. Herman Jones, resident at 3 Potter Place, in the town of Hillcrest, New Jersey, that, on the evening of November 1, he was in violation of a town ordinance forbidding the erection of a nonpermitted fixed structure in the open area between the residence and the street. The fine for such violation is in the amount of fifty (50) dollars for each day that the structure stood. The letter goes on to specify how the fine is to be paid.

"I think," says my father, "that, law-abiding citizen that I am, I ought to attend next week's Town Council meeting and restore my good standing in this town. And Callie, since you were the instigator of all this mischief, perhaps you ought to come with me."

On Monday night, when my parents and I enter the Town Council chambers, the room is nearly empty. We sit down in the front row. The minutes and the old business seem to take forever. I'm getting really impatient. Finally, the chairman asks if there is any new business.

My father starts to get up, but I tug at his sleeve.

"Dad, please, I'd like to do this."

"Yes, I think you ought to do it, Callie."

"Mr. Chairman . . ."

"Yes, miss?"

"I think the Town Council has made a mistake."

I can't believe I said that. The chairman can't seem to believe it, either.

"And you are?" he asks.

"Calliope Jones."

"Weren't you here in September? And, as I recall, weren't you only eleven years old?"

"Yes, sir. I still am."

The council members laugh.

"Well, Miss Jones, since you're *still* only eleven years old and since you're *still* not a taxpayer in this town, I can't allow you to speak. I believe that's your father sitting there. If there's a matter he'd like to bring before the council, I'd suggest that he be the one to do it."

"Please, sir, there is something that we'd like to talk about, but I'm the one responsible, so I think I should be the one to speak."

"Oh, all right. But please be brief. They're predicting snow tonight, and we'd all like to get home."

"Yes, sir. We got this letter in the mail." My father steps up beside me and hands me the letter. "It says that we were in violation of a town ordinance about fixed structures in front yards."

"Just a moment, Miss Jones." The chairman walks over to the secretary, who's sitting at the end of the table, says something to her, and waits while she finds the paper.

"Yes, Miss Jones, I have a copy of the notice right here. If you've come to pay the fine, you'll have to come to the office during business hours."

"No, sir, I haven't."

"You're not here to pay the fine. Well, then, please don't waste any more of the council's time."

I feel myself getting hot.

"I am *not* wasting the council's time. I believe the council is wasting ours."

My father puts a hand on my arm, trying to warn me, but I won't be warned. Or stopped.

"I beg your pardon, Miss Jones. Did I just hear you say that the Town Council is wasting your time?"

"Yes, sir, you did."

Now my mother is standing on my other side.

"This is a school night. I should be home doing my homework. And unless there's a really big snow tonight and school is going to be cancelled tomorrow, I'm going to be up really late doing it. But the real thing is, you're wasting *your* time. There wasn't any 'fixed structure' in our front yard on the night after Halloween. All the fixed structures were in the back, and there isn't any ordinance about backyards."

"As I understand it, there was an enormous metal monster in your front yard that night. Am I wrong?"

"No, you're right. Except it wasn't a monster, it was a dragon. But it wasn't fixed. You see, that's the point. The dragon moved. It rolled into the yard, turned around, and rolled out again. It did that three times."

"Ah, then you admit that there was a structure in your yard."

"Of course there was. But you're not *listening*."

Now my father is jerking my elbow. I know I'm going too far now, but I just can't stop myself.

"I've already told you. The dragon wasn't fixed. It rolled in and out. Like a lawn mower. Or—or a car in a driveway. So we weren't violating any ordinance, and I don't think we should have to pay a fine."

"One moment."

The chairman covers his microphone with his hand; the other members of the council gather around him. They all seem to be talking at once. The chairman uncovers his mike and looks at me.

"You say that the thing wasn't fixed, that it moved?"

"If you don't believe me, I can get witnesses who were there. They'll tell you."

"Calliope!" That's my mother. Out loud. I really have gone too far.

"Well, if the thing wasn't fixed, if it moved . . .

There isn't any ordinance regarding moving structures. Though I think we might have to draw one up. However, for now, the fine is vacated.

"But since you have brought this matter to our attention, there is something else that we ought to address—that display that you and your family set out the night after Autumn Fest. We've had a complaint: we've been told that the display was in rather poor taste, that there were a number of horrific figures, including the monster—excuse me, the dragon—which some people thought quite frightening. It seems that there were a number of children attending this performance. Of course, we can't tell your parents what kinds of activities they ought to be encouraging, but—"

"No, sir, you can't. My brother Jack would say that's a free-speech issue. And I'd say he's right. As a matter of fact—"

I'll never finish that sentence. My parents are whisking me out of the room.

Callie's Rules:

- Grown-ups will never admit you've won an argument.

· · ·

The next morning, when I carry my bowl of cereal to the table, there's a gray velvet box sitting at my place. I look over at my mother and father, but they suddenly get busy buttering toast or reaching for the milk.

I remove the lid, then the square of white cotton. Inside are two silver charms—a dragon with ruby eyes and a tiny heart.

Now everyone's watching me.

"A dragon, for my bracelet. And a heart. But . . . ?"

"The heart," my mother says, "is because you've shown such courage. Although"—now she stops and looks over at my father—"although you might want to work on not speaking out when you're angry."

"I know." I feel a little twisting inside me as I remember what I'd said the night before. "I guess I did get a little carried away. But it all just seemed so unfair."

"It was unfair," my father says. "And you did the right thing by speaking up for fairness. Next time, however, you might also want to be polite.

But there's still another lesson from all this that your mother and I think is important. The council passed an ordinance banning all fixed structures in front yards. We couldn't violate that ordinance, but you figured out a way to display the dragon and still obey the regulation. You made a mature decision, and we're proud of you for that. But your insolence last night was childish. You need to work on controlling your temper, Calliope.

"In any event, we were going to give you these two charms for your birthday, but since you're *still* going to be eleven for quite a few more months, we thought you should have them now."

I leap up and hug them both, then run out of the room so they won't see the tears in my eyes. When I come back, I'm holding my charm bracelet.

"Please, Mom, would you put the charms on for me?"

"I'll just go and get my smallest pliers. Be right back."

When my mother comes back, I ask her to put

the dragon on one side of the charm and the heart on the other.

"Thank you," I say as I fasten the bracelet. "You two are the best."

I'm hugging my parents when Polly comes in, dragging her blanket and rubbing her eyes.

"Callie," she says, "would you make my chocolate milk? You make it better than Mommy does."

She means that I put in more chocolate. I pour the milk and then the chocolate—lots of chocolate—into a glass. The chocolate sinks to the bottom, and I'm just about to start stirring it when a new thought pops into my head. There's no rule that says the milk and chocolate always have to be stirred together. Why can't you drink all the milk—the part that's good for you—first, and then spoon up all the chocolate from the bottom? Maybe it's okay that there are two separate parts. Maybe it's even better that way.

"Polly," I say, "I've just invented a new way to drink chocolate milk. Try it."

I pick up my backpack and my lunch.

"I'd better get going. I can't be late for school. It never did snow last night."

"Calliope." My mother stops me. "Wait, you're wearing the bracelet. You said you're not allowed to wear bracelets in gym class."

"That's the rule, Mom. But I think I'll find a way."

Callie's Rules:

• Even if you're telling yourself, "There's no way," sometimes you *can* find a way.

Naomi Zucker is the author of *Benno's Bear*, as well as several books for adults. She lives with her husband in Kingston, Rhode Island, where she's working on Callie's next adventure. You can visit Naomi online at www.naomizucker.net.